THE DYEDS OF MARCH

A KNITTING GAME MYSTERY BOOK TWO

HILARY LATIMER

To Joanie,

A true Criminal Knitter
and good friend,

Hilay Latiner

To Ande
For going down the rabbit hole with me

CHAPTER ONE

"Turn here, turn here, Wes!" Harry yelled, tugging on his arm as she pointed at the brightly painted, oversized mailbox leaning haphazardly over the road.

Wes dutifully slowed, turned on his turn signal, and pointed the nose of his SUV toward the long rutted gravel driveway, wondering for the hundredth time how she'd talked him into going to yet another "yarn" event. Considering how the last one had turned out.

"It's not a fiber festival," she'd told him earnestly when she'd first broached the subject. "It's a dye crawl."

"A dye crawl," he'd echoed, tilting his head just a little as he looked into her moss green eyes, not buying her declaration for a minute.

"Yes," and she'd beamed at him as if that explained everything.

"And what exactly does a 'dye crawl' entail?" he'd prodded.

She'd batted her eyelashes at him. "A lovely night at a picturesque bed and breakfast in rural Virginia."

So far, so good, he thought.

"Followed by a gourmet breakfast."

Better and better; he definitely loved a good breakfast. Which of course she knew, evil minx.

"And then, of course, there's the dye crawl itself."

"Of course," he'd echoed dryly, and she'd laughed and patted his jaw and told him that three well known dyers, who all happened to live near each other, had gotten together to open their dye studios to the public.

"And?" he'd queried because there was always an "and."

"And," she'd added, eyes dancing in excitement, "they're giving demonstrations on how they mix their dyes and do their dyeing."

Wes had to admit, that didn't sound too terrible. It might even be interesting. Especially if it included how they made the speckled yarn Harry was so fond of.

"But that's not all!" Harry had added, practically bouncing, "They're having workshops where we get to mix our own dyes and then dye our own yarn!"

Which, Wes thought, actually sounded like a lot of fun.

"They maaaaay also have yarn for sale," she'd added.

Somehow, he didn't think there was any "may" about it.

"Will there be another dead body?" he'd deadpanned, because there had been at the last yarn event he'd gone to with her.

She'd smacked his arm. "Don't be ridiculous! There's just going to be yarn. Lots of lovely yarn!"

And because Wes would do anything for Harry, of course he'd agreed to go with her. Which was why they were bouncing down this rutted gravel driveway on an otherwise perfectly lovely spring morning.

Wes was a large man, with cornflower blue eyes and blond hair that he wore longer on top and shorter on the sides. For some reason he wasn't quite sure of, it also had the curious tendency to be lighter on top, giving him the appearance of a person who spent a lot of time outdoors.

At the beach, according to Harry.

Which explained why she tended to describe him as either looking like a cross between a beach bum and a vacationing thug, or a surfing enforcer, much to his amusement. He was neither. He was a Federal Agent.

And okay, maybe just a little bit of a thug.

When it was needed.

"Harry, why are we the only ones here?" he asked, slowing as they got nearer to the empty parking area in front of the weathered barn that, Harry assured him, housed Grace Harper's studio.

"Probably because everyone else decided to start at Daphne's? But I didn't see the point since her workshop is the last one," she said with a careless shrug. "So, I thought we'd start here, at Grace and Favors. Well, at Grace's. Meredith Favor's studio is our next stop."

"Grace and Favors? Really?" Wes couldn't help grinning.

"I know, so cute, right?" Harry enthused. "And they have the loveliest yarns. Wait until you see their gradients!"

Oh yay—whatever those were.

Harry's eyes narrowed. "I heard that." She growled.

"What? I didn't say a thing!"

"You didn't have to. I heard you anyway."

Of course she had.

Pulling the SUV off to the side near the old barn, Wes killed the engine. Then he bit back a smile as Harry flipped down the visor so she could see herself in the mirror and started to fluff her hair.

It was such a 'Harry' thing to do, and Wes couldn't help the little grin that tugged at his lips as he watched her—his five-foot-five-inch sassy Irish girl, complete with flaming red curls, mossy green eyes and creamy freckle-dusted skin.

He hadn't been looking for love when they'd met, he'd been looking for his new apartment when he'd stumbled into hers by mistake. But love had a way of taking you unaware, and in the year since that momentous occasion, Harriett Flanagan had slowly started to fill up all the empty places in his heart he hadn't even known were there.

Happy with the way her hair looked, Harry turned her attention to her lips, muttered something under her breath, then dug through her cavernous handbag until she came up with her lipstick.

"Shimmer or Proudly Pink?" she asked, eyes twinkling as she held up the two containers for his inspection.

He tilted his head and gave the question its due consideration.

While Proudly Pink was one of his favorite colors on her, Shimmer plumped her bottom lip making it beg to be kissed and nibbled and—"Proudly Pink," he managed to grind out before his brain got any ideas about ravishing her in public.

Not that there was anyone about. Still.

In fact, the place seemed oddly deserted if you didn't count the crows sitting on the barn's roof watching them intently. Wes didn't, since he was still trying to drag his mind away from where it had been heading.

With a smirk, knowing full well what he'd been thinking, Harry serenely applied the glossy pink to her lips. He watched her trace their outline, then smack their full, lush plumpness together.

Damn woman. She knew exactly what she was doing to him.

"Staying or coming?" she asked, eyes alight with laughter, as she reached for the door handle.

"Coming," he told her. Not because he wanted to look at yarn, but because she'd promised him there would be "munchies," and his stomach was reminding him it had been hours since they'd left the city to drive up here.

And longer still since breakfast.

Throwing a saucy little wink at him, she began to walk toward the barn leaving him to trail after her, deliberately letting her hips sway, knowing he was watching. And how could he not with the way the slinky black material of her pants hugged every inch of her?

"Keep it up, woman," he growled, catching up to her.

She slid him a playful look. "Oh, I intend to," she told him, grinning, as he slid an arm around her waist.

Casting a quick glance around to make sure they were still alone he pulled her close, fully intending to kiss her.

"Behave!" she admonished, laughing as she wriggled out of his reach. Then, eyes alight and dancing, she ducked through the open barn doors ahead of him. And screamed.

All thoughts of kissing Harry's full pink lips fled as Wes launched himself through the barn doors after her.

CHAPTER TWO

"Wes!" Harry gasped. "She's dead!"

That was an understatement. The very dead woman on the floor had a pair of shears sticking out of her back.

A very large pair of shears, Wes thought, stepping in front of Harry to shield her from the grisly scene. His eyes swept the barn's interior as he slipped into FBI mode, gun in hand, without even thinking about it. But the killer was gone, though not long gone, he reflected looking back at Grace Harper's body.

She lay on the polished oak floor, hands on either side of her head, one higher than the other, as if she'd tried to catch herself as she'd fallen. Her legs were outstretched, the right knee slightly bent, her long green skirt caught up and bunched under it, revealing the butterflies that danced and fluttered gracefully in tattooed spirals from her ankle to her knee, droplets of blood scattered incongruously amongst them.

Her head was turned away from them, for which Wes was grateful.

He could still vividly remember the first pair of empty eyes he'd ever looked into, and he didn't wish that memory on anyone.

Especially Harry.

"Close your eyes, babe," he told her softly before moving away from her toward the dead woman, mindful of the crime scene all around him. Crouching beside the body, he checked for a pulse not surprised when he didn't find one. But he checked, because you never knew, and there was always hope . . . until there wasn't.

Eyes sweeping over the scene again, he frowned as he stood up and holstered his gun. Blood was splattered and splashed in a wide arc across the floor and over the skeins of yarn that hung neatly on the barn's left-hand wall. A smaller pool had spread from beneath the dead woman's body.

The spatter, he understood, cast off from the stabbing. But the splashes . . . He shook his head. Blood didn't splash.

Then, moving back just as carefully toward Harry, Wes eased her outside and held her close as she burrowed into his arms. He hated that once again, murder had ruined a yarn event for her.

What was wrong with these knitting people? Couldn't they kill each other privately, without an audience?

He knew he was being ridiculous. They probably killed each other in private just as often as any other segment of humanity, especially since this particular murder didn't look premeditated.

No, whoever had killed Grace Harper either hadn't known about the yarn event or hadn't cared about it.

A crime of opportunity then, more than likely.

And a crime of rage. Whoever had killed Grace Harper had been *angry*.

Damn! The yarn event!

Glancing quickly toward the end of the driveway and the road beyond it, Wes gave a mental sigh of relief, since both were still mercifully empty. But they wouldn't remain that way for long. The knitters would be coming, and there were things he needed to set in motion before they got here—like closing off the driveway so no one else could pull up it and calling 9-1-1. And he needed Harry's help to do it, since he couldn't leave the crime scene unguarded.

He pressed a gentle kiss against the side of her head, hating that he couldn't give Harry any time to grieve. But he needed to close the scene off, and quickly. "Red?" he said softly. "You doing all right?"

"Yeah. I'm fine," she said resolutely, only the barest tremor in her voice giving her distress away, her words slightly muffled since her face was still pressed against his chest. Then, taking a deep breath, she pulled back enough to see him. "I'm *angry* more than anything," she told him, eyes blazing.

"I know, babe," Wes answered, gently wiping away an errant tear that was trickling down her cheek. "I'm angry too," he paused for just a second before adding, "but right now, I need you to do something for me."

"Anything," she said quickly.

"I need you to take the SUV and go block the driveway," he said, cupping her cheek. "No one gets through unless they're law enforcement. Or the coroner." Although, more than likely, it would be a while before the coroner got here, and by then the police would have taken over the scene.

She nodded sharply. "I can do that."

"That's my girl," he said, brushing his lips across her forehead.

She clung to him for just a second longer before she took a step back, straightened her shoulders and dashed another stray tear from her cheek. "Yes, I can do that," she said again more firmly.

"Thank you, Red," he said simply, handing over his keys.

"Find out who did this, Wes," Harry told him fiercely. "No one deserves to die like that."

No, he agreed, they didn't.

CHAPTER THREE

"9-1-1, what's your emergency?" the voice asked briskly.

"This is FBI Special Agent John Smith. I'm at Grace Harper's dye studio. She's been murdered."

For a moment, the line was silent before the dispatcher said, "Oh my god. Are you sure?"

"Very," Wes said, and then the dispatcher remembered her job.

"I have patrol units heading your way," she told him before she repeated, "oh my god!" Then more softly, "Who would murder Grace?"

That was the question, Wes thought turning back to look at the crime scene again. In the distance, he could already hear the rise and fall of a police car's siren getting steadily closer. Now that's what he called a rapid response. Although on reflection he realized the patrol car had probably already been in the area.

Standing just inside the doorway, Wes let his eyes slowly

sweep across the interior of the barn, taking in everything. First impressions of a crime scene were crucial to an investigation. Not that he was planning on investigating anything, but he could pass them on to whoever would be.

The coppery smell of blood hung heavy in the air, mingled with the sharp tang of vinegar and something else he couldn't quite put his finger on.

The vinegary smell came from the yarn for some reason he couldn't quite remember. Harry had most likely told him why once, but he'd forgotten.

The coppery smell was self-explanatory, but the third odor was barely there. A wisp of something harsh. Hairspray maybe? Or . . . bleach? He shook his head and let his eyes drift on.

The barn had probably housed a tractor once. But that had been a long time ago, before the pale pine walls had been varnished to make them smooth. Now they were a backdrop for the skeins of yarn that hung four deep on wrought iron hangers to the left of the shop door and across the adjoining wall. A kaleidoscope of colors marred now by splashes and splatters of blood.

Too much blood, Wes thought again, looking them over thoughtfully. The splatter was one thing, but the splashes were just—wrong.

He turned his attention to the rest of the shop.

To the right of the door, directly opposite the yarn, brightly colored bags with Grace & Favors' logo lined a tall potter's bench under a window behind a makeshift wood counter that had been a door once. A stack of neon bright tissue paper lay to the side of them, ready and waiting to wrap up purchases that were never going to happen.

On the counter itself, an iPad stood, ready to check out customers. His eyes lingered on the iPad for a moment before moving on.

But nothing looked out of place. It simply looked like Grace had been walking across the barn when someone had stabbed her. Someone she had trusted. Someone she hadn't been afraid to turn her back on.

Someone who had come through the sliding doors at the back of the barn maybe? Doors that at first glance he thought had led outside. But what if they didn't?

What if the barn was larger than it looked and had been divided into the shop upfront and the studio behind it, because, he suddenly realized, there was nowhere to dye yarn in this tiny shop. Which meant the dye studio was someplace else.

Like behind those doors.

Had Grace and her assailant both been back there before something had happened? An argument. A scuffle. And Grace had tried to run away?

And what if there was someone still back there, hiding?

His hand went for his gun, before it stilled again. He could hear multiple sirens now, their discordant wailing bouncing off the hills around him, closer than before. If he went back there now, alone, he ran a good chance of getting shot by some over eager deputy newly arrived on the scene.

Better to wait and go in with them.

Not that he thought they'd find anyone back there, but they needed to clear the building before they could put his talents to better use.

Except there wasn't going to be any "they" he told himself, as he stepped back outside of the barn again. This wasn't his crime scene.

It probably wasn't the anxious young officer's who was approaching him now, either. The deputy's eyes darting from the partially opened barn door to Wes and then back again. His hand hovering over his holstered gun.

Okaaay then. Flipping his badge case open, Wes held it up so the man could see it. "FBI," he added for clarification.

The officer swallowed hard and bobbed his head. "Clara said," he told him.

Clara? Wes thought, before realizing that was probably the 9-1-1 dispatcher.

"Is, uh, is she really dead? Grace? Miss Harper?" he hurriedly amended, making no attempt to verify it for himself. Anxiety bleeding out of his every pore.

Someone he'd known then. Lovely.

"Yes," Wes answered bluntly.

All the color fled from the young man's ruddy cheeks, his plain square face crumpling in on itself, hands fisting at his sides. To Wes, it looked like he was trying not to cry.

Swearing silently to himself, Wes did the one thing he did

not want to do: took control of the situation, because someone had to.

"Deputy?" he paused, waiting to be filled in.

"Uh, Clay. Dale Clay," the young man stammered, swallowing hard again as he tried to pull himself together.

"Deputy Clay, was Grace Harper married? Did she have any children? Anyone who might be in the house still?" Because if anyone was, making sure they were safe took precedent over searching the dye studio for someone who wasn't going to be there anyway.

The officer's eyes slid past Wes to the old farmhouse that stood just beyond them.

The concrete walkway that led up to it was cracked here and there, a product of time rather than neglect, since the house itself boasted a new coat of white paint. Weed-free flowerbeds lined the walk, bright green shoots reaching for spring pushing up through the mulch someone had laid to protect them from the vagaries of winter weather.

Clay's eyes widened just a fraction before he shook his head. "Shouldn't be no one in there. Except her cat, Maisie."

His eyes slid toward the barn doors, before he swallowed hard a third time and blurted, "I'll just go take a quick look 'round. Make sure nothing's been disturbed." And almost stumbling over his feet in his hurry to get away from the barn, he suited actions to words and bolted for the house.

Wes just hoped the man had enough sense not to touch anything as he did his walk-through.

Movement caught his eye. Turning his head, Wes saw a second squad car pull up alongside his SUV which Harry had parked across the driveway. A moment later she let it through and as it headed towards the barn, Harry rolled the SUV back into place, blocking the driveway again.

"Clay, is that your boss?" Wes called out hopefully, to the man's retreating back.

Pausing only long enough to look over his shoulder, the deputy shook his head. "No, that's just Jeb," he called back.

Turning back to the cruiser, Wes sighed as a man even younger than Dale Clay got out of it and looked nervously around. At the exact same moment, Wes heard Clay yell, "This is the police. I'm coming in!"

Whipping his head around, Wes was just in time to see Clay pull his gun, reach for the front door's handle, and go in.

Dear god, why me? he thought. Two green officers and a cat who was probably going to get shot. Making a quick decision he turned quickly back to Jeb, fixed him with a hard stare and barked, "No one goes into the shop except your boss or the coroner. Got that? Including you."

All they needed was a green officer's vomit adding to an already complicated crime scene.

"When you have back up, the dye studio behind the shop needs to be searched." He called back over his shoulder, already jogging toward the house after Clay.

The deputy had left the front door ajar. Pulling his gun, Wes slipped through it into a large, airy living room which had probably been two rooms when the house had been built. Now a giant TV with a gaming system dominated one end of the room, with a bright blue sectional in front of it. While the other end of the room boasted a wood-burning fireplace with a cream-colored love seat opposite it, flanked by matching armchairs. A patchwork quilt, in every color of the rainbow, lay draped across the back of the couch to add a splash of color to that end of the house.

Remodeled, Wes's brain told him, having watched countless episodes of those home makeover shows with Harry, as his eyes swept the space looking for Clay—or anyone else.

But it was the deputy's broad back he saw disappearing through the opening across the room into a bright sunlit kitchen. A second later, the man's voice, an octave higher than normal from fear, suddenly bellowed, "Hands in the air!"

Lengthening his stride, Wes burst through the doorway after him just as a familiar voice yelped, then yelled, "Damn it, Dale! Look what you made me do! And quit pointing that gun at me!"

CHAPTER FOUR

A petite, blue-haired teen, resplendent in ripped black jeans and a black T-shirt with Grace & Favors on it in a neon rainbow, stood just inside the back door, eyes blazing. A pastry box was cradled in her arms, and another lay where it had fallen on the kitchen floor. The lid was partially open, and a lone glazed donut was just finishing its wobbly roll before coming to rest against the center island.

"What. Are. You. Doing?" she yelled at the startled deputy. "Did you think I was breaking in?" Twin spots of color marred her cheeks, her breathing faster than normal. "How many burglars leave donuts for god's sakes?"

Wes burst into the room. The girl's eyes widened in shock, before surprise and delight raced across her face. "*Muscles?* What are you doing here?" she exclaimed.

Holstering his weapon, Wes had to stifle a grin at her nickname for him. Something the outspoken, sarcastic teen had coined the first time they'd met. And judging from the way she'd just been tearing the hapless deputy a new one, Janine Cavanaugh hadn't changed a bit since then.

"I could ask you the same thing," he answered, since she lived in D.C.

Her lips curved up into a grin. "Yeah, except this is a knitting event, and I knit." She shot back, "Unless," she added, grin widening, "you've taken up knitting?"

"No," Wes said firmly, cutting her off, to her obvious amusement. "I have not taken up knitting."

"Unlike your pretty partner," she smirked.

He'd give her that. His partner, Fountain Rhodes, did in fact knit, although badly by all accounts.

"Is he here too?" she asked peering behind him as if she thought Fountain's lanky figure would magically appear.

"No, I came with Harry."

She gave a little squeal, practically bouncing with happiness. "Yay! I love Harry! She's the coolest—but," she paused, frowning, "that doesn't explain all the gun waving. Unless someone else has been murdered," she added flippantly.

It was how they'd met, at another knitting event. For a brief moment her uncle, whom she lived with, had been a suspect in his ex's murder until Wes and Fountain had cleared him.

They'd been friends ever since.

"Wait—you two know each other?" Clay interrupted, giving

Wes some much needed breathing room to decide how to tell the teen that yes, that was exactly what had happened.

"No," Janine said, rolling her eyes, "I always call random stacked guys 'Muscles.' "

"Janine, behave." Wes said trying for stern, though judging by Janine's smirk, failing miserably. She'd been the same way when he'd first met her, all snark and grit, and he'd liked her immediately because of it. "And, yes" he added, answering Clay's question brusquely, since how they knew each other was none of the man's business.

"So, back to what *you're* doing here," Wes asked again.

"Delivering donuts for the dye crawl?"

Her "duh," was unspoken as she set the box she was holding on the center island. Then, bending to pick up the one she'd dropped, she only hesitated a moment before grabbing the donut that had rolled away and putting it back in the box it had fallen out of.

"What?" she asked, catching his raised eyebrow. "The ten-second rule totally applies here." She licked the glaze off her fingers. "It hasn't been more than ten seconds since I dropped it, has it?" Her smirk was firmly back in place.

Since there was no good way to answer, Wes just shook his head.

"Back to why you're here, *again?* You didn't come all the way from D.C. to deliver donuts," he prodded.

She snickered. "No. I'm here because *someone* thought a great way for me to spend my spring break would be by interning with Meredith Favor."

Ah. That sounded exactly like something her Uncle Aiden would think, since Wes had no doubt that he was the *someone* in question.

"Doing what?" he asked curiously. Janine had once told him she thought she might like to follow in her uncle's footsteps, and since Aiden Cavanaugh was a fairly well-known knitting designer, not a dyer, he wondered why interning with one might be useful to her.

"I'm learning all the ins and outs of yarn dyeing so I can 'visualize' how yarn can be manipulated. Like, gradients as opposed to speckled, that kind of stuff, which all comes into play when you're designing something. And, yeah, playing in the dye pots has been kind of cool," she acknowledged. "That's Merry's place, up there."

Through the open back door, Wes could see a large field and another old farmhouse on the rise above it. A well-worn path was clearly visible leading from one to the other through the tall amber-hued wild grass.

"So that's Meredith Favor's place," he mused.

Janine rolled her eyes. "Um, yeah? Pretty sure that's what I just said."

Interesting. He didn't think it would take longer than a few minutes to cover the distance between them . . ..

He made a mental note to comment on it to whomever

ended up being in charge. Afterall, business partners were always suspect when their partners were murdered, until they were cleared. And that path was a little too convenient to be ignored.

"So, why are *you* here" Janine asked, still in snark mode, "and what was with the whole waving guns around bit? I mean, really —what was *with* that? Although, speaking of guns, do you sleep with yours or something? You always seem to have it on you."

"I keep it under the pillow," he told her, even though he didn't, because that would be foolish. "And yes, I carry it, always." Which he did. "Even to knitting events."

"Because you never know when you're going to need to shoot some little old lady because she dropped a stitch, right?"

When Wes didn't fire back a funny answer, Janine's grin faded away, eyes darting between the two men as the silence lengthened.

"Wes? *Has* something happened?" she asked. Uncertainty and a little fear crept into her words. When he hesitated a moment too long, again, her eyes widened slightly as she put two and two together. "Something's happened to Grace, hasn't it?"

Unsure of how well she'd known the woman, Wes kept his voice soft as he said, "I'm sorry, Jan. But Grace Harper's dead."

"That—that's not possible," Janine gasped. "Meredith was just talking to her!"

"What! When?" Wes asked urgently.

"Um . . .not long ago?" she answered, eyes wide in shock.

"Maybe an hour or so?" "What happened?" she asked, clearly shaken. "Was it a heart attack? Oh god, I need to call Meredith. No, I need to get out to the barn. People will be coming and—"

Wes shook his head. "The barn's a crime scene, Jan, no one's going in there, and I don't want you calling anybody. Not before they've been officially notified."

Wes heard Janine's sharp intake of breath at his mention of a crime scene. "Oh no," she half whispered. "She's been murdered, hasn't she?"

"I'm afraid so, yes," he said softly. He hated that she was caught up on the edge of a murder investigation, again.

Janine shook her head. "But that doesn't make any sense. Who would want to kill Grace?"

Then her eyes flew open wide, and in a flurry of arms and legs she pushed away from the counter she'd been leaning against and exclaimed, "The dye crawl, Wes! It's probably already started! I mean, there will be people all over the place, at Meredith's and Daphne's and trying to get in here, and there's a killer running around someplace! We need to stop it!"

Wes chose his words carefully. "I don't think there's any way to stop it, and I don't think anyone else is in danger, either."

Janine's eyes widened as she realized what he was saying. "Shit, you think the killer was someone she knew."

"More than likely."

"But—what possible reason could anyone have to kill Grace?"

"I don't know," he answered honestly.

"But you'll find out, right? I mean, you're going to help with the investigation?"

Wes shook his head. "It's not my jurisdiction," he told her. "And I can't just go poking my nose in without being invited in by whoever's in charge here."

"That would be me, and consider yourself invited," a new voice said from directly behind Wes.

Turning, Wes met a pair of faded blue eyes in a weather-worn face. He was square jawed and clean shaven, just a trace of gray in his brown hair. The man's nose sat a little off center, having met a fist or two at some point in his fifty odd years.

"We just don't have anyone on the force right now with the experience to deal with something like this, besides me and Clay here, and since I'm broken right now," he said humorously, nodding at the crutches that were supporting him, "and Clay is being my eyes and ears, I'd be happy to take any help the FBI can give. Sheriff Don Weaver," he added, extending his hand. "And I'm assuming your Special Agent Smith?"

"I am." Wes said, shaking his hand. "John Smith, but everyone calls me Wes. I'd be glad to help."

The sheriff laughed. "Smith and Wesson, I like that." He said, catching on to Wes's nickname immediately.

"Your lady friend told me you were up here, once she was sure I had the 'authority' to enter the 'crime scene,' that is," he said, making quotation marks around the words, both of which the sheriff clearly found humorous.

That sounded exactly like Harry, especially since the sheriff was dressed in jeans and a T-shirt, over which he'd hastily thrown on a sheriff's department windbreaker. She wouldn't have let the man through on just his say so, not dressed like that, not without making him prove who he was first.

Oh shit! Harry. She was not going to be happy with him right now. From the sound of things, she was still guarding the driveway. "I'm sorry, but I need to—"

"Your friend is fine," the sheriff told him, a lazy smile on his face. "I've got a deputy guarding the end of the driveway now. Harry's over next door with Grace's nice neighbor lady, Ellen Montrose."

The name conjured up images of a sweet, gray-haired lady with lacy doilies on the arms of her couch and the smell of moth balls in the air.

Wes let out a sigh of relief.

"The woman was really shaken up to hear Grace had been killed. Apparently, she was supposed to help out during the yarn thing."

Janine gave an unladylike snort, muttering something that sounded like, "I just bet."

"Problem?" Wes asked, biting back a grin at her obvious dislike of the "nice neighbor lady."

The teen rolled her eyes. "Amongst other things, she doesn't *approve* of me," she answered, gesturing at her lip ring and blue hair.

"Anyway, your Harry volunteered to take Miss Montrose home and sit with her for a bit," the sheriff went on, eyeing Janine but not making a comment.

"You seriously need to go rescue her," Janine said urgently. "Sooner rather than later."

The sheriff snorted. "I don't think she was expecting to be 'rescued' any time soon, seeing as how she took her knitting with her."

That also sounded like something Harry would do.

Then, with a wink at Janine, the sheriff went on, "As for locking the scene down from crazed knitters, besides the deputy at the end of the driveway, I have a pair of cars blocking either end of the road that leads down here, which should stop anyone who shouldn't be here from getting through.

"I also sent patrol cars around to let the other dyers know there's been an—incident—here and that Grace wouldn't be participating in the dye thingie," he said to Wes.

All of which Wes approved of. The man might not have anyone in his office who knew how to work a homicide, but he did know how to stop anyone from panicking and how to close down a crime scene thoroughly.

"An incident?" Janine howled, outraged at his choice of words.

"Best not to start a panic by yelling 'murder' from the rooftops," the sheriff said dryly.

Then, noticing the boxes of donuts on the center island, the sheriff asked, "Were these for the yarn thing?"

When Janine nodded, he sighed and said, "It would be a damn shame if they went to waste." Opening the lid on the box nearest him, he took out the donut that had rolled across the floor and with a happy sigh bit into it.

And neither Janine, nor Wes, nor Deputy Clay said a thing.

CHAPTER FIVE

"It's a cliché, I know, but nothing beats a donut," the sheriff said, munching away happily. He paused for a minute when he was done, eyed the open box, then, with a sigh, reached out and closed the lid.

He was a medium-tall man with broad shoulders. His pale blue eyes were framed by laugh lines, though there was a certain shrewdness to them too that told Wes he was a seasoned officer. Wes also didn't think a second donut would have hurt him any, but the sheriff was clearly a man who knew his own limits when it came to both food and law enforcement.

"So, how do you want to do this?" Weaver asked, turning his gaze from the donuts to Wes. "I realize you're here to do the yarn event, but any help you can give would be much appreciated."

Wes nodded, thinking things through. He didn't mind missing out on parts of the dye crawl to help catch a killer. But he had no intention of making Harry miss out on anything, not if he could help it.

"Unless you have someone else you'd rather send, I'd just as soon do the initial interviews," Wes said carefully.

He didn't want to step on the man's toes, despite the fact he'd been the one who'd invited him in. But he thought he should be able to wrap up any interviews fairly quickly. Unless there was a line out the door of people who'd wanted to kill Grace.

"Sounds good to me," Weaver agreed amiably.

Moving away from the conversation, Deputy Clay reached for a can of cat food that had been left out on the island, obviously intended for Maisie's bowl, a fact the orange cat was broadcasting loud and clear.

"In that case, I think I'll start with Grace's business partner, Meredith Favor," Wes said, thinking he could take Harry with him. That would make her happy, since she'd be able to poke through the woman's sale yarn while he interviewed her. "She ought to be able to give me a list of family and friends, as well as any romantic partners she might have had so I'll know who else to talk to."

A sudden, loud clang made everyone jump, as Clay dropped the bowl full of cat food, the sound ricocheting across the kitchen.

"Maisie!" he yelled, pushing the cat out of the way. "Dang it, look what you made me do!"

The cat didn't care. She'd jumped down from the counter and was busy eating what splattered food she could get to.

"Leave her be," Weaver said, as his deputy looked around wildly for something to clean the mess up with. "She'll lick it all up. No point in having a break down over it." Turning back to Wes, he continued their conversation as if nothing had interrupted it.

"Between you and me, I'd rather you do whatever interviews you think need doing. I suspect a Federal Agent showing up on the doorstep packs a bit more of a punch than the local sheriff or a wet-behind-the-ears deputy. Not to mention the fact I'm supposed to be keeping off my feet. Tore a ligament snowboarding," he added, grinning. "Although it's probably just as well I stay here and keep an eye on things, anyway.

"We had a huge turnover of officers recently," he explained. "A lot of my seasoned deputies retired when the county commissioners decided they needed to pass a physical fitness test. So now, except for Dale here, this new lot have never handled a homicide, and he's only worked one. It's not like we have more than one or two every five or six years.

"So, you taking care of the interviews means I can stay here and observe. See who can handle what, for next time."

Because there was always a next time, sadly.

"The boys did all right, poking their heads into Grace's studio to make sure there was no one in there. But they need to see how the CSI's work a murder scene, so they don't go blundering through one, messing up evidence. They can handle a robbery, but a murder scene is a whole other game."

That it was.

"Works for me," Wes agreed.

"Or I could go," Clay volunteered, suddenly. "It would give me a chance to get more experience interviewing." The barest hint of pleading was in his voice.

Weaver rubbed his chin, thinking it through before he shook his head. "As good of an opportunity as it would be, since you're my senior deputy I need you here with me. Matter of fact, as soon as we finish up here, you should probably head on down to the barn and make sure Jeb isn't screwing up anything."

Clearly unhappy with his boss's decision, there was nothing the man could do except agree.

"I think I should be heading back too," Janine said, edging toward the back door, ready to make her escape.

"I have a better idea," Wes told her, his smile all teeth. "I'll have someone drive you back to Meredith's right after I ask you some questions, seeing as how you're here now."

"There's no need, Wes—she lives right up there!" the teen objected.

Wes nodded. "She does," he agreed, "but you're still getting a ride."

He didn't want her to be the one who told Meredith that Grace was dead. In fact, if there was a long way around that the deputy could take, that would be even better. It would give him a chance to pick up Harry first and still beat Janine to Meredith's.

She huffed out a breath, rolled her eyes, and said, "Fine." She knew when she was defeated. Then, grumpily added, "What did you want to ask me about?"

"Let's start with the phone call you mentioned. The one Meredith got from Grace. You said it was maybe an hour ago? Do you remember what you were doing when she called? Something that would help nail down the time a little more accurately?"

Something he could start building a timeline of events around, because Grace Harper hadn't been dead long when they'd found her.

Rocking back and forth on her heels, thinking hard, her eyes suddenly flew open wide. "Yes! I remember that we'd just finished eating breakfast! So—a little after eight, I think?" She turned to look at Clay and for a moment Wes thought she was looking for him to confirm that, before he realized she was just watching him playing with the cat, now that it had finished cleaning up the mess he'd made when he'd dropped her breakfast.

"All right, good. And how do you know it was Grace that Meredith was talking to?"

"Because Merry put the call on speaker, since she was washing the dishes."

Better and better.

"Do you remember what they talked about?"

Out of the corner of his eye, Wes saw Clay look up and stare at Janine intently. Good, Wes thought, maybe something she'd overheard would mean something to him, while meaning nothing to Wes.

She hummed for a second before saying, "Yeah, Grace was

complaining about Ellen, the neighbor lady, being underfoot again, and then she asked when I'd be down with the donuts. But I was in and out, feeding the birds, so I didn't hear everything, and then I went to take a shower," she said apologetically, "so I have no idea what else they said. I mean I could still *hear* them talking, if you know what I mean? A kind of faint murmur in the background, just not the words."

Fair enough.

"Did you see Meredith again, before you came to bring the donuts down here?" he asked casually. His gaze drifting out the door again as he considered what else to ask her.

"Um, yeah. Right before then, actually. She was just heading out to the studio and got the door for me."

He nodded absently. The path through the field catching his attention again.

"You didn't see anything when you were walking over here, did you? A car, maybe, or a person?"

She frowned, thinking hard. "No," she said finally. "But you can't see the front of the house or barn from back there. You can only see the backs of the houses, although there were a couple of cars on the road by Meredith's. But they could have been coming or going from anywhere. As far as people?" She shook her head. "I didn't see anyone."

It had been worth a shot. It wasn't like there were security camera footage he could look at. He'd noticed the lack of cameras reflexively when they'd first driven up to the barn. But, on the other hand, being out here in the country, Grace probably hadn't seen the need for any.

"So, are we done here now? 'Cause I should really get going," Janine asked, easing toward the back door again. "I'm supposed to be helping Meredith in her shop right now."

"All right," Wes agreed, clearly surprising her. "But you're getting a ride, remember?"

That won him a little whine and an eyeroll. Both of which he ignored.

"Come on—let's see if, Jeb, was it?" he asked the sheriff.

"Jeb'll do," The sheriff agreed, eyes twinkling in amusement at Janine's obvious annoyance.

"Let's see if Jeb can give you a ride now," Wes said with a grin of his own.

"God, that's such a waste of county resources!" Janine complained, trudging out of the kitchen after him, the sheriff and Clay bringing up the rear.

This time, the sheriff laughed out loud. "Good thing they're mine to waste then. But better to know you got back safe than to be sorry."

"What could possibly happen to me walking across a field?" Janine grumbled.

"Let's not find out. Afterall, there's a killer lurking around somewhere."

That shut up the teen entirely.

"So, how well did you know Grace?" Wes asked, as they

made their way toward where Jeb leaned against his patrol car, watching them as they walked toward him.

She shrugged. "Not well. I mean, I see—saw her at the fiber shows sometimes, the big ones. So, I knew who she was. But Merry and Grace split up the smaller shows they went to, because there are, like, a million of them. There's simply no way you can go to all of them and still have time to dye yarn too."

That made sense, Wes supposed. He knew from Harry that Virginia and North Carolina between them had a slew of shows, only one of which she'd managed to drag him to so far. So he had to assume Pennsylvania and Baltimore and all points north did too. But it also meant that Grace would have had her own set of people she hung out with, then. Different people, more than likely, than the ones Meredith knew.

"She seemed nice enough." Janine added, quietly. "Always smiling. One of those people who was really happy doing what they were doing." She sniffed. "God, this is all just so —pointless!"

Murder generally was.

CHAPTER SIX

"Is this really necessary?" Janine whined as they came to a halt in front of the patrol car.

"Yes, it is. Now get in." Wes opened the rear door. "And Jan, I need you to promise not to let Meredith know what's happened. That's not really something someone should find out in a text or over the phone."

And much to Wes's relief, Janine got into Jeb's patrol car with only a roll of her eyes and a snarked—"Fine, I promise not to call, text, or send smoke signals up to Merry. Good enough?"

"Good enough," he agreed. And it was, because he knew Janine was a girl who kept her word.

"She's a live wire, is that one," the sheriff said, watching as Jeb turned left at the end of the driveway. Then, with a little laugh, he added, "And I see Jeb's taking the scenic route, something I'm guessing you asked him to do?"

Wes nodded. He wanted to tell Meredith himself.

"Oh, and Dale," the sheriff added, "that thing about keeping this quiet? That goes for you, and everyone else too. No calling or texting anyone about Grace having been murdered. I want this crime scene shut down tight as a drum. Heads will roll if I find out anyone's been talking. Make it so," he added in a perfect parody of Captain Jean Luc Picard.

"So, I'm guessing you sent the girl the long way back to make sure Meredith Favor hears the news from you first?" the sheriff asked, watching as Dale stopped briefly to talk to the deputy who'd taken over "barn door watching" duty in Jeb's absence.

"That is the plan."

"In that case, you'll be wanting to turn right instead of left out of the driveway," Weaver told him, laughter in his voice. "Then take another right at the stop sign at the top of the road. Her driveway's up a few hundred feet. Shouldn't take more than a handful of minutes to get there. If you leave now, you should arrive a few minutes ahead of that little blue-haired girl."

That suited Wes perfectly. Fishing his phone out of his pocket, he sent a quick text to Harry.

Wes: Done here—need to go talk to Meredith Favor, then the other dyer.

The other dyer, who Harry was a huge fan of.

Daphne Goshart? she replied promptly.

Wes: Yeah. Her.

Harry: Meet you in two.

Wes couldn't help grinning. He'd thought from the start that the whole point of the weekend was so Harry could spend time fangirling over the Goshart woman by taking her dye class, and he had every intention of seeing that Harry did just that.

Now, if the nice neighbor lady had told Harry some juicy gossip about Grace, that would just be icing on the cake. Law enforcement officers loved nosey neighbors for a reason. He hoped Harry had milked her for all she was worth.

"So, tell me all about our nice old neighbor lady," he said, once Harry had climbed into the car and was fastening her seat belt.

Harry giggled. "Well, first off, she's not old. Maybe forty something?"

Not what he'd been expecting.

"And predictably, she was pretty freaked out."

Yeah, hearing someone you knew had been murdered had a tendency to do that.

"Which is how I met her in the first place," Harry went on, barely taking a breath. "Once I got relieved of driveway duty, I headed up to the barn looking for you. But you were off somewhere, sleuthing," she added, sliding him a sideways look, a grin on her face.

"I do not sleuth," he told her, biting back a grin of his own. "I investigate."

"Po-tay-to, po-tah-to," she shot back, eyes alight with laughter. "Anyway, somehow our Miss Ellen had made it all the way to the barn doors without noticing all the police cars, and when she did, she totally flipped out."

Wes looked over at the doors in question. How was that even possible?

Two deputies stood off to the side of them, out of the way of the CSIs decked out in hazmat suits who were coming and going out of the barn itself. Two cruisers and a white-paneled van sat haphazardly in the graveled parking area in front of it. How on earth could anyone have missed all that, or even made it that far?

"I have no idea. Don't ask," Harry said, reading his mind. "I guess she was just really focused on getting to the barn. Or maybe she had earbuds in, or—maybe she lied and just wanted to know what was going on."

That last one, Wes thought, seemed the most likely.

"How did she get by you?" he asked curiously, slipping the car into gear and heading down the bumpy driveway.

"She didn't. She came through the backyard." Wes caught her raised eyebrows when he shot a look her way.

Seriously? Had no one thought to go around back to keep people out? Apparently not if Harry's expression was anything to go by.

With a nod at the deputy playing guard dog at the end of the driveway, Wes eased the SUV out into the road, thinking the sheriff must have been thrilled to hear that.

"So, did she have any juicy gossip on Grace?"

"Not that she shared. But to be honest, she was still pretty freaked out. Alternating between 'why would anyone kill Grace' to 'my god I could have been killed too if I'd gone back to the barn just a few minutes earlier.' "

Which, Wes thought, was about right. Shock at the death of a friend, and relief it hadn't been her.

"What made her think the murder had just happened?"

Harry frowned. "I think she just assumed."

"She didn't mention seeing anyone dressed all in black running through her garden, did she?" he teased. Eyewitnesses, by and large, were notorious for giving inaccurate descriptions of people fleeing crime scenes.

"Nope. Not so much as a single boogeyman sneaking through her peonies," she giggled. "Not that I pushed her much. Mostly I just got her settled in on her couch with a nice cup of tea and her knitting. Give it an hour or so, and I'm sure she'll remember something."

Wes nodded, no doubt. Either real or fabricated.

"She's on my list of people to interview. Right after I talk to Meredith and old what's her name," he added, biting back a grin, knowing that was going to drive Harry crazy.

"Daphne Goshart," Harry repeated in exasperation. "Pay attention!"

"I did the first time. I just like the way you say her name. All prim and proper," he told her, snickering when she smacked his thigh.

"Oh, you!" Then, a grin dancing across her own lips, she added, "You're an idiot."

"But you love me anyway, right?" he asked, taking her hand

in his and giving her his best puppy-dog eyes, laughter bubbling in his chest.

"You wish," she told him, imperiously, shaking off his fingers before collapsing in a fit of giggles. "You're ridiculous," she told him, eyes bright with laughter.

Pulling up to the stop sign at the top of the road, he leaned over and stole a kiss.

CHAPTER SEVEN

There were a surprising number of cars parked in front of Meredith Favor's dye studio. More than Wes had expected. Some, he noted, even had out of state plates. He hadn't realized how popular a dye crawl would be. Then again, Harry *had* managed to talk him into coming, and that had involved a three-and-a-half-hour drive from D.C.

Excited chatter drifted on the breeze as Wes got out of the SUV. As he turned to say something to Harry, the words died in his throat when he caught the look of longing on her face as she watched a particularly exuberant group of people push through the double doors of Meredith's shop and disappear inside, loudly speculating on who was going to buy the most "goodies."

God he was an idiot, he'd forgotten to tell her he expected her to go play while he talked to Meredith. "Hey, babe? Go play. There's yarn in that building calling your name."

"What?" She turned and stared at him, her leaf-green eyes almost comically wide in surprise. "But—"

Coming up beside her, Wes gave her a little kiss on the cheek. "But nothing, Red. I'm the sleuth, remember? It's not that I don't need my Watson," he added, when she opened her lips to protest. "It's just that I don't need her until later. Until after I have some facts to run by you. So go play. Just keep your ears and eyes open for anything anyone says that seems out of place."

He watched as a million thoughts streamed across her face.

"Okay. I can do that," she said, finally, nodding. "No one knows she's dead, right?"

"No one except for the killer. And Janine," he added, as the patrol car she was in pulled up and disgorged the disgruntled teen.

"Janine?" Harry asked, eyes widening as she caught sight of the teen, then shot Wes a look that spoke volumes. He knew he'd have some explaining to do later.

"I am seriously annoyed with your boyfriend," Janine told Harry, hands on her hips, glaring in his direction as she came up beside them.

Something Wes thought Harry might also be.

"I'm pretty sure he had that deputy drive me all over the county just so he could get here first—like he didn't trust me not to say anything or something. But you, I'm happy to see." She added, accepting Harry's hug, clinging on to her a little longer than Wes expected.

"I trust you completely," Wes told her sincerely, once they

parted. "I just wanted Harry to be here when you got back," he lied, coming up with something he thought the teen would believe.

Janine stared at him suspiciously for a moment before the angry look on her face slid away and tears filled her eyes. She blinked hard and sniffed.

"Okay." Then more quietly, she added, "Thank you."

"Are you okay, sweetie?" Harry asked softly.

Janine took a wobbly breath before nodding, and then very quietly asked, "Did you just get here?"

"Yes," Harry answered.

"Then Merry doesn't know yet, does she?"

"No, hon." Harry brushed some stray hair off Janine's face. "Wes was just about to go tell her."

Janine sniffed again, then, taking a deep breath, said, "She'll be in the shop. I'll, uh, introduce you." Taking a deep breath, she led them across the parking area to the bright blue painted cinder-block building and into what appeared to Wes to be the seventh level of hell.

Women shrieked and chattered and called out to one another, waving coveted skeins of brightly colored yarn above their heads in triumph as their friends cheered them on. If he hadn't been there for a reason, he would have turned tail and run.

Janine dove right into the throng without a backward glance, and, grabbing Wes's arm, Harry dragged him along in her wake, as she followed after her.

"Janine, what's going on?" an anxious voice blurted, thick with equal parts fear and relief when the speaker saw the teen.

Wes had the quick impression of a short, thin woman, dark hair pulled back in a loose braid, before she pulled Janine into the corner behind the checkout counter—a tiny oasis of quiet in the whirling maelstrom around them.

"A deputy was here just a little bit ago," the woman, whom he assumed was Meredith Favor, went on, her voice frantic with worry. "He said something had happened to Grace and that her part of the dye crawl had been cancelled, but he wouldn't tell me *what* happened, and I can't reach her on her phone, and now I just saw another deputy brought you home—what's going on?"

Though her voice had been pitched low, Wes could still hear the edge of fear and worry in it as he stepped behind Janine into the tiny space, thankfully free of crazed knitters.

He cut in before Janine could answer. "Why don't I tell you, Miss Favor?"

Meredith Favor turned wide, worried dark brown eyes on him, her lips parting into a shocked "O" when she saw the sheer size of him. And for a moment, Wes thought he saw a brief flash of fear. But whether that was from his size or something more nefarious, only time would tell.

"This is Wes Smith," Janine told her, keeping her voice equally low, "and that's his girlfriend, Harry Flanagan," she added, gesturing toward Harry, who had stepped behind the makeshift counter and was chatting with a group of ladies waiting to check out there. Stalling them until Janine could take care of them. "They're friends."

Meredith looked at her in confusion.

"He needs to talk to you, Merry, about what happened. He's ―"

"The police. Thank god. Yes," she cut in, in relief, "what's happened?"

"Mer, no, he's not," Janine interrupted. "He's a Federal Agent. Except he's not here as a Fed. Not, exactly," she rushed on. "He's just helping out because the sheriff asked him to. And he really needs to talk to you."

"Grace, is she okay? No wait―not here. Up at the house maybe?" she added, glancing around her packed shop.

"That would be perfect," Wes agreed.

"I've got this. Go," Janine told her, giving her a little push toward the door, before turning away and stepping behind the counter, where Harry was just putting a skein of bright green speckled yarn into a neon pink Grace & Favors bag.

"One skein of Frog Pond twist sock in colorway Rib-it," Harry said, handing her the buyer's credit card, before moving out of the way so the teen could ring up the sale.

"Thanks," Wes heard Janine say gratefully under her breath, fingers already flashing across the screen of the shop's iPad as she entered the information to complete the sale.

"Just give me a shout if you need any help," Harry told her, giving the teen a little hug. "But in the meantime, you can point me toward the Butterfly Collection."

And Wes caught Janine's little smirk as she glanced across the shop before saying, "Over there," waving her hand toward the thickest part of what appeared to Wes to be a rugby scrum.

With a quick glance at Wes, her eyes alight with excitement, Harry didn't think twice before diving into the fray.

CHAPTER EIGHT

Meredith Favor ushered Wes through the door of her farm-house, into a front room almost the exact duplicate of Grace Harper's, right down to the wide opening on the back wall that led into her own sunlit kitchen, leading Wes to think that they'd either helped each other remodel or had hired the same person to do it.

In the front room, a pair of orange cats lounged on a neon green, crushed-velvet love seat—litter mates to Grace's Maisie maybe? Another couch, in a clashing pink fabric, sat caddy corner to the love seat. The walls had been painted a neon orange and were hung with neon abstract framed posters. Wes felt like he'd stepped into a Candy Crush game.

"Agent Smith?" she asked, anxiously collapsing onto the edge of the love seat, dislodging the cats who'd been sleeping there. "Please—what's happened?"

With matching "rowr"s of displeasure, the cats leapt up onto the sofa and glared at Wes while he looked around for a place to sit, as if daring him to move them again. He opted for an eye-jarring lime-green overstuffed armchair, and, satisfied, the cats stretched out and went back to sleep again.

"Please?" Meredith begged, her voice quavering. "All the deputy said was that there'd been an incident, like it wasn't anything serious. But I can't reach Grace. She's not answering her phone. What's happened? Is Grace okay?"

"I'm sorry," Wes said, "there's no good way to tell you this, but Grace Harper's dead." His words hung between them, suspended in the absolute silence that followed.

"She—no—she can't be!" Grief chased after the words that tore out of Meredith's throat. "I talked to her just—just a little while ago."

Pushing up from the love seat, she took a half step forward. "I need to see her—I—" With a little sob she collapsed back down again, reaching for a box of tissues that sat on an end table beside her, cluttered with paperbacks and knitting needles and yarn that oozed out of a project bag, trailing what appeared to be a half-worked sock behind it.

"Oh god. Oh god," she moaned. "What happened? It couldn't have been a car wreck—she wouldn't have been driving anywhere—and it couldn't have been a heart attack. Was it? No, that doesn't make any sense—" Her words rambled, disjointed, colliding into each other until they came to a jumbled stop.

"She was murdered," he said bluntly. "I'm sorry for your

loss." He hated the words, knowing how empty they always sounded.

Meredith's eyes opened wide, her mouth slack with shock.

Her hand went to her throat. "No, no, no, no," she whimpered, shaking her head, back and forth. "No. You're wrong. Who'd want to kill Grace? Are you sure? How . . . how . . . *why?*" she implored finally.

The million-dollar question, to which he had no answer.

She cried for a little bit, scooping up her kitties who had run back to her when she'd started to weep. Then, the shock and the aftermath wore off, and she sniffed, blew her nose, and wiped away the tears that still streaked her cheeks. "Who—who?"

Wes shook his head. "We don't know. Yet."

The word hung between them, and he saw her shiver, before she snuggled one of the cats and held it close for a minute, the other one meowing piteously until she reached out and held it closer too.

He gave her another minute. He could afford that. Then, swiping at her cheeks again, she cuddled her cats closer and half whispered, "How can I help?"

"If you feel up to answering a few questions?"

She sniffed, then barely audibly said, "Yes." Then clearing her throat, she tried again, her voice coming out louder this time as she said, "anything I can do to help you find out who did this. But please first—how—how –"

"She was stabbed."

"Oh god." Dislodging the cats, she wrapped her arms around

herself, rocking back and forth while tears streamed down her face again. Then taking a huge, ragged breath, she dug down deep, blotted at the tears on her face, sat up straight, and said, "Ask me anything."

Wes took her words at face value.

"Let's start with your whereabouts. Can you walk me through your morning?"

She swallowed hard, throat working, eyes sliding away from his as she reached for another tissue and blew her nose noisily. Giving herself time to think things through.

Huh, Wes thought. Well, that was interesting—she was already hiding something.

"I woke up earlier than normal because of the dye crawl. I'm not much of a morning person, so I'd set my alarm. That's how I know I woke up at seven o'clock. Though I, uh, might have lain in bed for just a little bit after."

She said the words quickly, almost running them together, as if she couldn't get them out fast enough. As if maybe they weren't completely truthful, and she wanted to rush past the not-quite-truthful part as quickly as possible.

"Then I," she paused, fingers twisting the tissue to shreds. "Oh! Then I came into the kitchen and made coffee."

He nodded encouragingly when she glanced up.

"Then I went back to the bedroom, brushed my teeth, and threw on some clothes." The routine mindless, normal. Something she did every day without having to think through it, the words coming out relieved instead of rushed. Unlike the way she'd told him about the start of her day: the part that Wes suspected hadn't been quite truthful.

One of the cats wormed its way back into her lap, and she dug her fingers into its fur gratefully, while the other one pushed up hard against her thigh.

"What happened next?"

She startled. Her thoughts having drifted away. "Ummm. I—I"—a flush crossed her cheeks—"I made breakfast for Janine and me." She glanced at him for just a second before her eyes skittered away again. Hiding something else, Wes noted.

"Then," she frowned, thinking, before tears filled her eyes and spilled over. "Then Gr—Grace called," she said on a sob. "I was doing the dishes, and I was annoyed because I had to dry my hands in order to answer it." The sobs came harder then. Guilt eating at her for having had such a thought when now she'd never be able to talk to Grace again.

Wes gave her a few moments before asking, "About what time was that?"

She gulped in air and grabbed another tissue to blow her nose again.

"I don't—I don't know." She came to a stumbling pause.

"You were doing the dishes," Wes prodded. "So you'd finished breakfast."

"Yes." She nodded. "So it must have been about eight or eight-fifteen, maybe? I don't *know* exactly." She ended on a whine.

Close enough to what Janine had told him.

He made a mental note to check in with Sheriff Weaver when he was done here, to see if the coroner had an estimated time of death yet. But he was willing to bet it had been somewhere between eight-fifteen and eight-forty-five, which gave their killer a very narrow window of time to have killed Grace.

"Do you remember what you talked about?"

"Um, one of our neighbors, the business, and"—she dug her hands into the scruff on the larger cat—"and, um, when Janine was going to bring some donuts over to her for the dye crawl." Her eyes slid away from his again, and he wondered what she'd left out.

He let silence drift across the space between them for a minute. Watching as she fidgeted, first with the cat and then with another tissue, before asking, "Was anyone else in the kitchen with you when Grace called?"

Meredith stilled for just a second. "Janine," she said faintly, then swallowing hard, she added, "I put the call on speaker so we could talk while I finished cleaning up, so I'm sure she heard us."

He gave her a reassuring smile. "You're doing great," he told her, and the tension in her face eased just a little bit.

"What did you do next?"

"I took the compost out, then I just stood there in the backyard for a bit, just breathing." Her voice trembled a little. "Then after a while, I went back inside and took a shower, and after that I went out to the studio."

"And about when was that?"

"It was about, um . . .ten to nine when I headed to the studio, I think? No, wait. I stopped and talked to Janine first. She was in the kitchen, getting ready to take Grace the donuts, and *then* I went out to the studio."

Wes nodded. Janine had told him the same thing.

"I, um, need something to drink," she said, getting up abruptly. "Can I get you anything? Water, tea?"

"No, I'm good. Thank you."

Meredith gave him a strained smile and hurried the few feet into her black-and-white kitchen, complete with retro 1950's turquoise appliances. She hadn't realized he'd followed her until he said, "Tell me about Grace. Did she have a boyfriend or any recent exes?"

The glass she'd just reached for fell through her hand and shattered in the sink.

CHAPTER NINE

"I'm fine! I'm fine," Meredith told him, breathing hard, when he leapt to her side. "I'm fine, really. It's all fine," she repeated, fishing the glass fragments out of the sink. "I have plenty of other glasses. It's just—this whole thing—and then you startled me."

Tossing the bits of broken glass away, she took another glass out of the cabinet and carefully filled it with tap water.

"I'm sorry," she said, folding herself back down onto the love seat again a few moments later. "You asked about a boyfriend. She didn't have one. Not lately," she told him staring down at the glass of water clutched firmly in her hands.

"And no angry exes either, then? Nothing like that?" he prodded.

She shook her head. "No. Nothing like that."

Pity. An angry ex would have given them a direction to head in.

"Tell me about Grace & Favors."

Her head shot up at the sudden shift in his questioning.

"I'm not sure I understand. What do you want to know about it?" she asked, eyes narrowing, suddenly cautious.

Well, well, well.

"You were partners, right? So, what happens to it now that Grace is dead?"

Her eyes flew open wide. "Oh no! We weren't partners like that," she said, shaking her head vehemently. "Not really." Then she softly added, "It's complicated."

"Enlighten me.".

She swallowed hard.

He waited.

"Grace & Favors isn't a company—not the way you're meaning." She took a sip of water, then set the glass down on the end table, pushing aside her knitting, buying herself some time while she thought things through. "It really just started as a way for us to be able to afford—things," she said finally.

"What kind of things?"

"Pretty much everything. Booths at shows, hotels, yarn, dyes, even our advertising. Everything was just so expensive, and we were barely making ends meet. Then one day we got to talking about ways we could make more money, and the obvious answer was to go to more shows. But we just couldn't afford to. And then suddenly it was like this lightbulb went off.

"It was so obvious.

"Instead of going to the same shows and paying for separate

booths, we needed to go to *different* shows and take each other's stuff! But when we looked into it, the shows wanted to charge us extra for sharing. So we decided to pretend we were one company and it kind of snowballed from there. But we never made it a legal entity, like an LLC or anything. We just split all our costs right down the middle.

"The only time we did shows together was when we went to the really big ones, because they're total bedlam."

Bedlam, he thought, was putting it mildly, having experienced firsthand how crazy a fiber festival could be.

"Like Coastal Carolina?" he asked, naming the one he'd been to, which also happened to be the largest fiber festival in the South.

She nodded. "Yes."

Not one of the booths he'd visited when he'd been there with Harry, though he was pretty sure Harry had not only visited their booth but had bought at least a bag's worth of yarn from them.

"Last year's event was especially awful," she went on with a shudder, "because one of the designers was killed there. Murdered."

Wes knew, since he and his partner, Fountain Rhodes, along with Harry and Janine, had been instrumental in finding the man's killer.

"And now Grace has been murdered too," she wailed, "and we're never going to get to do another show together ever again." The idea brought on a fresh flood of tears.

Wes waited patiently until she was down to sniffles before asking, "So, if you're not actually business partners, what happens to Grace & Favors now?"

Meredith blew her nose noisily. Then lifting one of the cats back into her lap, she hesitated for another moment before saying, "We weren't business partners but . . .." Her voice trailed off.

"But?" he prodded.

She sighed heavily, fingers carding anxiously through the cat's fur, before she cuddled it close to her. "We agreed, years ago, that if anything ever happened to the other one, that the survivor would get full rights to the name and all the other person's business assets. It's not like any of our family wanted to inherit a bunch of yarn or dye, anyway. So it made sense to make sure the other one of us got it. We even put it in writing, notarized and everything, so there could never be any doubt as to what we wanted."

Well, that was interesting.

"Who else knew about the agreement?"

"No one," she said positively. "It was private and nobody's business. We never thought it would amount to anything, anyway." A tear trickled down her cheek. "It was never *supposed* to amount to anything."

But now it had, Wes thought, keeping his face carefully neutral, and it placed Meredith Favor firmly on his suspect list as someone who had something to gain.

"Do you have a copy of your agreement handy?"

She shook her head. "Not here, no. It's in my safe deposit box, and the lawyer has one. Freeman, Greene, and Burke."

He nodded, making a mental note to ask Sheriff Weaver to get a copy of it and a copy of Grace's will, too, if she'd had one. Afterall, he only had Meredith's word for it that Grace's yarn and dyes were all that had been left to her. Had she owned her home? Did she have money in the bank? He needed to know what else, if anything, Meredith stood to gain from Grace's passing.

"Just a few more questions. I know you need to get back to your customers."

She shook her head. "I don't know if I can do this," she half whispered, swiping at fresh tears, her gaze fixed on the living room floor. "Grace was my best friend. How do I just pretend everything's okay?" she asked him.

She couldn't. But what he said was, "Can Janine run the workshop for you today instead?"

"Ye—es. But"—she sniffed—"those people out there came to see me." Scrubbing at the tears that had started trickling down her face again, she added, "And I can't let them down. Grace would have hated that."

She took a deep, steadying breath. "What else did you need to know?"

"Did Grace have any enemies? People who were angry with her?"

"No." Meredith shook her head. "Everyone loved her."

Right. Why did people always say that, especially after the

person in question had been murdered? He gave himself a mental shake. It was time to wrap this interview up, and he only had one question left. Getting up as if to leave, he took one step away, then paused and turned back.

"One last question: you wouldn't know who Grace's last boyfriend was?"

Better to check he had nothing to do with her murder than to take Meredith's word for it.

Meredith froze, caught in the act of pushing the cat off her lap, when her cell phone chimed, signaling a text message.

"It's Janine. I need to go. She's swamped," she said, practically leaping up in relief. "If we're done, that is?"

But before he could answer, her eyes slid past his to the large picture window. They flew open wide as she exclaimed, "Oh my god, where did all those people come from?"

And turning to look, Wes was as surprised as Meredith. The parking area out front was completely full, while more cars lined both sides of her driveway.

"Go," he told her, opening the front door and ushering her through it. Someone else could answer the question of who Grace's boyfriend had been.

No one, on the other hand, had to answer what Harry had been doing. She was loaded down with bags full to bursting when she met him at the SUV.

"I got it!" she said, beaming as she handed them over to him. "Now I can make that sweater I've been wanting to make!"

Diving into the nearest bag, she pulled out a prewound cake of yarn and waved it excitedly at him.

It was cream colored with pale green speckles. Peering into the bag it had come out of, Wes saw four more skeins, each one like the first except they gradually darkened in color, all with some variation of speckles until the last one, the darkest one, had cream-colored speckles.

While Wes had no idea which of the million sweater patterns Harry owned this yarn was fated to become, he did know it was going to suit her perfectly.

She gave a happy sigh, patted the yarn, then slipped it back into the bag.

"Where to next?" she asked as he stowed her purchases in the back seat.

"Daphne Goshart's," he told her, and Harry gave a little squeal before biting her lip. "I shouldn't be this excited that I'm going to meet her, should I? Not with poor Grace being dead."

"Babe, you be as excited as you want to be," Wes told her. "What happened to Grace has nothing at all to do with you."

"I know. It's just—"

"Bad luck that someone else was killed at another yarn event we came to." Pulling her into his arms, he gave her a chaste kiss on the corner of her mouth. "Now let's go meet Daphne Goshart."

Which earned him another little kiss, and a breathless, "Yes!"

CHAPTER TEN

Daphne Goshart was chic and sophisticated in her pale pink skirt, matching jacket and cream silk blouse, a sharp contrast to Meredith in her tie-dyed Grace & Favors T-shirt and thread-bare jeans.

Wes took one look at Daphne and whispered to Harry, "I think we're in the wrong place."

"Shhh," she hissed back, smacking his arm, "don't be ridiculous and she'll hear you."

Closer to fifty than thirty, Daphne had bright blue eyes and silver-gray hair cut short and styled meticulously by a hairdresser who, Wes was sure, had never set foot outside of the city. Any city. Pick one.

And she was English.

He hadn't expected that either. She had a posh accent to go with her posh looks. All she was missing was a string of pearls.

"Hello! Come in and welcome. Don't be shy. There's room for

everyone!" she called out, her smile bright and genuine, as if she was truly delighted that they'd come to visit her.

Painted a deep, dark green with large cream panels where her sale yarn hung, her shop was warm and inviting.

"Look around—there's lots of lovely yarn you can purchase, and if you're interested in doing the workshop later this afternoon, there's a sign-up sheet over there."

"Over there" turned out to be an antique lectern tucked into the bay window Wes had noticed when they'd first driven up.

"Okay, fangirling big time over here," Harry murmured, as he signed them both up, much to Daphne's obvious amusement.

"This one's a keeper," she told Harry, coming up beside them, laugh lines crinkling at the corners of her eyes as she patted Wes's arm and then introduced herself, as if they didn't know who she was already.

"Daphne Goshart," she said, "and you are?"

Wes had to bite back a snort as he heard Hermione Granger's voice in his head asking the same question the first time she'd met Harry and Ron.

"Harry Flanagan," Harry gushed, "and this is Wes Smith."

"Hello, Harry, Wes, I'm so glad you could come, and that you're going to play with us. And thank you, Harry, for bringing some sorely needed eye candy," she added soto voce, cyes twinkling. "It's not every day we get a lovely footballer signed up to play in the dye pots."

"Federal Agent," Wes corrected softly, "And, while I do want to play in the dye pots' later this afternoon, is there somewhere we can talk, now? Privately?"

Daphne's eyes widened slightly. "Oh! Has something else happened? No—never mind. Of course it has. That's why you want to talk in private. Give me just a minute to make sure Peter knows I'm stepping away, and we can go up to my office."

Her eyes swept around the shop's interior before coming to rest on a young man who was talking to a trio of excited women across the room. Wes put him somewhere in his late twenties. A tall, dark haired man who turned when he felt Daphne's eyes on him, raising an eyebrow in question when their eyes met.

Daphne pointed to Wes and Harry, then herself and then pointed upwards. The young man, Peter, looked them over carefully before nodding.

"Right then, I've got a little sitting room I call my office upstairs, where we won't be disturbed. Will that do?"

"That would be perfect," Wes said. "Thank you."

The sitting room turned out to be as warm and cozy as Daphne's shop downstairs. Painted a deep, dark rose it boasted two floral chintz couches and a pair of chestnut-colored leather armchairs.

A small kitchen ran along the back wall. Bookcases, jammed full of both hardback and paperback books, stood sentinel along the walls on either side of the room. While notebooks and pages painted over with broad strokes of color lay scattered across a long rectangular farmhouse table that took up the far end of the room in front of a wide window with a sill covered in potted plants of every size and color.

"I'd offer you tea or coffee, but I think I'd like to hear what this is about first," she said, gesturing toward the couches, "in case this calls for something stronger. I know there's been an 'incident' at Grace's. A deputy came by and told us earlier. But if the FBI's involved, I'm thinking it must be something more serious? Is Grace all right?" she asked looking back and forth between Wes and Harry.

"No," Wes answered bluntly. "She's dead."

For a moment, Daphne just stared at him, shocked. "Oh no! How? What happened? I mean she's only what, twenty-eight or nine? That poor girl." Then she stilled, searching Wes's face, sharp eyes reading what he wasn't saying. "She's been murdered, hasn't she? That's what you're not saying. And that's why you're here."

Wes nodded. "She was, and yes, that is why I'm here. I'm assisting the sheriff in his inquiries."

"Well, thank god for that. Oh no, that's not what I meant. Sheriff Weaver is most likely a knowledgeable police officer, but his deputies are as green as the hills." She paused for a minute, then shook her head. "Murdered? That doesn't make any sense. Who would kill Grace?"

Then, standing up abruptly, she asked, "Tea, coffee, or brandy? I'm afraid it's an old fall back of us Brits in times of trouble, and now I think I know why. It gives us something to do while we deal with the shock of hearing bad news. And don't say 'nothing'—we have a Keurig, so it's no bother."

"I'd love a cup of tea, in that case," Harry said honestly. "Earl Grey if you have any."

"I'm British. Of course I have Earl Grey," she said, amused. "Agent Smith? If you don't like tea, we pretty much have any kind of coffee imaginable, and a few no one's ever heard of except for my trendy young staff."

"A Dunkin Donuts coffee would be perfect if you have any, thank you. Nothing in it, just black."

Daphne nodded, slipped a pod into the Keurig, then filled a copper kettle and set it on the stove to boil.

"Now," she said, turning back around to face them, "tell me what happened. Never mind," she added, throwing up a hand with a sheepish shake of her head. "You want to know where I was this morning, first. My father was a DCS—Detective Chief Superintendent," she clarified. "You'd think I'd remember how these things go. What time frame are we talking about?"

A no-nonsense woman, Wes thought, with nothing to hide, which he'd expected.

"Between seven and nine a.m.," he answered, though it seemed, from what Meredith and Janine had told him, that it had been closer to eight-thirty or eight-forty-five when she'd been killed, but better to air on the side of caution.

Bringing a tray over to where they were sitting, Daphne set it on the table and let them help themselves as she settled onto one of the couches, teacup in hand. A wisp of steam rose above the rim.

"Let's see, at seven a.m., I'd just sat down to breakfast up here with Peter, China, and Adam—the other lovely young people on my staff. And while I'm not fond of early mornings, Peter likes to have 'team meetings' before an event so everyone knows what they're doing.

"We had scrambled eggs, bacon, bagels with cream cheese, and smoked salmon. Except for China, who had one of those green smoothie things. All spinach and kale and chia seeds, or something.

"I think it was probably very nearly eight a.m. by the time we'd finished eating and tidying up. Adam and China headed down to the shop to fuss, and Peter and I did a quick lap through the studio to make sure everything was ready to go for this afternoon's workshop, after which I came back up here to chill out for a bit until people started arriving, and Peter stayed downstairs."

"Good," Harry said, clearly relieved.

"I take it that means I'm not a suspect, then?" Daphne asked, smiling.

"No," Wes agreed. He'd thought from the beginning that it was unlikely, seeing as how her studio was roughly fifteen minutes away from Graces. Even if she'd killed Grace the minute the phone call had been over, it would have been cutting things close to get back, cleaned up and be ready for customers—especially if any had shown up early. And now he knew she had a staff to sneak past too? All but impossible.

"But you have questions, I think. What would you like to know?"

"How well did you know Grace?"

Daphne took a sip of her tea, then nodded. "I suppose 'not well' isn't going to help any. So let me back up and explain how I met her in the first place."

CHAPTER ELEVEN

"I split my time between the US and England. Not only so I can personally attend as many fiber shows as possible in both places, but to regenerate. I get a different vibe here in the States than I do in Little Hibblethwaite on Mur." A smile crossed her face. "We have such funny names for our towns.

"Anyway, when I'm in England a majority of my work is for the fashion industry. Coming up with color palettes for commercial knit wear—that kind of thing, not that I don't create colorways for yarns we sell to knitters, because I do, but that's not my main focus when I'm there.

"But, when I'm here, that's all I do. A much-needed balm for my soul. The fashion industry is ridiculously cutthroat. The indie dyer industry is more backstabbing."

That was an interesting choice of words.

"Not literally," she shuddered. "More in the vein of people copying your ideas or just plain being nasty." She paused, eyes on Wes's face. "And I've said something that caught your interest . . . oh no!" Her eyes flew open wide. "Please tell me Grace wasn't stabbed to death."

"I wish I could."

"God, how awful . . . Or, how apropos."

Wes raised an eyebrow.

"The Ides of March," Harry said softly. "Wes, today is March fifteenth. You don't think—"

"No," he said with certainty. "I don't."

Grace Harper's murder had been more of a crime of opportunity than anything else, and the date had had nothing to do with it, whatsoever. It was pure coincidence.

"Well, that's a relief. It would have been rather macabre, otherwise," Daphne noted. "But you think it was someone she knew," she added sadly. "Which brings us back to how well did *I* know her.

"We weren't really close, not the way friends are. I'm afraid. It was just happenstance that I bought this house. I didn't have any real criteria for a location when I started looking around for something permanent. I used to do these long-term leases while I was trying to decide where I wanted to be. America's so *big*.

"Anyway, the only thing I really needed was to be near a college town, because they're vibrant and eclectic and have young people looking for internships," she added wryly. "I finally decided I liked this area the best. Virginia or North Carolina—they remind me the most of home, I think.

"About ten months or so ago, Peter and I flew over to look at a couple of places. He's my PA, not my lover, you naughty man," she added, laughing, having caught the little glance he'd shot at Harry.

"I have children older than he is—with my second husband, who is a lovely man and to whom I am still married. The first husband was a terrible mistake when I was very young and much too foolish, to answer your unspoken question."

With a fond little smile, she added, "You might even meet him tonight after the workshop—we do a little wine and cheese thing—which is why I like to do events in the late afternoon.

"Then again, maybe not," she said, sighing, "since he's deep in the bowels of the thriller he's currently writing."

Wes blinked, suddenly making the connection. "Wait. You're married to *Edgar* Goshart?"

"Ooooh, whose going all fangirl, now?" Harry teased, knowing Edgar Goshart was one of Wes's favorite authors.

"That would be fan*boy,* and no, I'm not," Wes disagreed, lying manfully.

Daphne laughed. "I'll see what I can do about getting him to come so you can meet him. But he'll probably want to pick your brain about some technical matter, I'm just warning you."

"I'd be happy to help, not fangirling!" he added when Harry poked him.

"Anyway," Daphne said, getting back on track again, "while I was looking around, this place came open. There's another house on the property, farther back behind that lovely thicket of lavender and butterfly bushes, which made it the perfect place.

Somewhere to live and somewhere to play. When the realtor told me there were other dyers in the area, that clinched it.

"It took about six months to renovate both houses, and we moved in right around your Thanksgiving holiday because Edgar wanted to experience what it was like to live in 'snow' for his novel. We don't get much in Little Hibblethwaite."

So they'd moved in a little over three months ago, Wes figured doing the math in his head.

"I think we were still moving boxes in when Meredith came around to introduce herself. I met Grace and her boyfriend a few days later."

Wes sat up a little bit straighter. Her *what?*

"Grace's boyfriend or boy friend?" he asked, just in case he was jumping to the wrong conclusion.

"Oh, definitely boyfriend. A police officer. No, wait, they're called deputy sheriffs here, aren't they?"

"You wouldn't happen to remember his name, would you?" Wes asked carefully.

"Um," Daphne tapped a rose-colored nail against her lip, eyes staring into space. "Dale something . . . Dale Clay, that was it!"

What? Wes leaned forward, eyes intense as he asked, "You're sure that was his name?"

"Yes, positive and, that means something to you, doesn't it?"

"I met him today," Wes said blandly, running his hand through his hair and giving the part on top a good tug while thinking, Well, well, well. Dale Clay had some explaining to do.

"Not surprising, really," she said nodding. "I think the county only has something like six deputies in total. Not nearly enough for the area they're covering. But I expect Sheriff Weaver will fix that. As soon as he can find officers who can run a city block without having a heart attack."

And Harry couldn't help snorting at that.

"Ah, so you heard about the new requirement," Daphne said, smiling back. "And quite sensible too, I might add."

"What about your staff? Did any of them know Grace?"

"I think China and Adam knew her. At least in a sort of 'nod your head when you see them out and about,' kind of way. They're only here in the afternoons, after their classes are over, and on Saturdays too. And it's not like she came over very often. Probably only a handful of times when we were planning the dye crawl.

"Of course, Peter *did* know her. He was here the first time she came by."

"When you were unpacking?"

"Yes. I think he was quite taken with her right off the bat, and not very pleased she had a boyfriend. I think he might have asked her out if she hadn't. And, of course, he saw her every time she came over after that, since we were hammering out things for the dye crawl, most of which we ended up dumping on his shoulders to sort out. There are certain advantages to having a PA," she added with a wink.

He'd have to take her word for that.

"I'm sorry I can't be much more help. But I really didn't know either one of them very well. I'd seen them at shows, of course, when I was over here. But shows are hectic, and you tend to only socialize with people you know. So I was thrilled when they suggested getting together and doing a dye crawl, to be honest. I thought it might bring us closer together."

"How long ago was that?" Wes asked curiously.

"Not long after I moved in, actually. Probably not more than a few weeks? I think they might have already been batting the idea for one around. Anyway, we did a slew of online advertising, and the response was amazing. People loved the idea of a dye crawl, and with the added classes, it was fairly unique.

"We even got a good deal on hotel rooms over in Charlottesville for the people who had to drive too far to be able to go home overnight. That was the one logistic we really struggled over, since the people taking our workshops would have to come back the next day to pick up their projects. We couldn't really send them home with yarn dripping all over the place.

"Oh dear," she added suddenly. "Should we cancel the workshop?"

Wes shook his head. "Not unless you want to."

Daphne sighed. "I'll seem like a ghoul if I don't, and yet, all these people are here already."

"It would be better if you didn't," Wes told her. "We don't want a general panic if the news gets out that Grace has been killed. Right now, people are probably just assuming she fell and broke her leg or got ill. Something like that."

Daphne nodded, her sharp eyes roving over his face. "You think it was someone she knew, don't you?"

"More than likely," Wes agreed. He didn't see any point in hiding it.

"God, what a mess. I don't envy you. If there's anything I can do to help—tea, brandy, a quiet place to think things through—just let me know."

Smiling, it was Harry who said, "Thank you."

"And now, I have a question for you." Daphne leaned forward slightly. "Did you sign up for my workshop just as a way to meet me?"

"No!" Harry said, answering again. "You're the reason we *came* to the dye crawl! So I could take the class with you, and Wes said it sounded like fun, so he thought he'd take it too!"

"Then Sheriff Weaver didn't call you in to help with the investigation?"

Taking Harry's hand in his own and giving it a gentle squeeze, Wes shook his head. "No. It was more a right-place, wrong-time scenario."

"What Wes isn't saying is I was the one who found Grace," Harry said quietly.

Daphne's eyes flew open wide. "Oh, my dear, that's —horrible!"

"Yes, it was," Harry agreed in a small voice, because it really had been. She'd only had a glimpse, but she'd seen the shears sticking out of Grace's back and the blood splashed about.

"Which is why I want Harry to still do all the fun things we were planning to do, especially your workshop. Which probably sounds cold and uncaring—"

"Not in the least," Daphne interrupted. "You weren't planning on finding a dead body or getting pulled into the investigation. No, I quite agree. In fact, what if I give you a sneak peek now of my dye studio?"

"Oh, I'd love that!" Harry enthused. "What do you say Wes? Do we have time to do that?"

"We have all the time in the world, babe," he told her.

Afterall, it wasn't like Dale Clay was going anyplace.

"Excellent! It'll give you a chance to step away from the investigation and catch your breath for a moment too," Daphne said, leading the way back downstairs and through a door at the back of her shop.

"Not to mention the fact that Father always said being distracted by something silly or inconsequential always helped his subconscious sort through the information he'd gathered while he wasn't hovering over it or dissecting it. He said sometimes simply playing a game of Go Fish! or Hide and Seek gave him the most startling revelations."

"Here's to a startling revelation then," Wes said, not that he'd had to step away from the investigation to have had one. Now the question was, why had no one told him that Dale Clay and Grace Harper had been dating?

CHAPTER TWELVE

Daphne's dye studio looked like something that Disney might have dreamed up. Every surface was pristine and sparkling as if waiting for a kindly witch to appear and make magic happen.

"And this is where the magic takes places!" Daphne said, echoing the words that had been in Wes's head.

Gizmos and whirligigs sat on two massive islands that ran down the center of the studio, gleaming under giant copper glad lights, while on the nearest island, lobster pots sat in rows—wait, what? Wes blinked, but those were quite definitely lobster pots sitting there.

"My god, this is—amazing," Harry breathed beside him, trying to take in everything at once.

Wes wasn't sure "weird" wasn't a better description, but what did he know?

On closer inspection, he realized the lobster pots were sitting on gas burners, which were set into black counter tops, racks of pasta tongs standing beside them. Okaaay. Weird just got weirder.

Especially as several massive farmhouse sinks lined the wall directly behind the burners, boasting state of the art touch faucets. Beside them stood a row of gleaming commercial-grade steamers like you saw at high-end buffets to keep the food warm.

If he hadn't known better, Wes would have thought he was in the kitchen of some upscale restaurant. Except the items on the second island belonged in a potions class.

Glass beakers and measuring cups, plastic pitchers and wooden racks filled with eye droppers stood in clusters down the length of it. Ceramic containers holding an array of what appeared to be measuring spoons and stirrers sat in easy reach of each cluster.

There were also several plastic gallon jugs with powder inside them labelled "citric acid" stacked at either end of the counter alongside boxes of non-latex, powder-free gloves and, inexplicably, boxes of Saran Wrap. Under the counter, on open shelving, Wes spied a dozen more jugs of the citric-acid powder.

Behind the island, on the far wall, rough wooden shelves had been fixed to the white-shiplap walls. Jar after jar filled with powders in every color imaginable sat on them in a carefully orchestrated manner.

"It looks like a cross between a chem lab and a seafood restaurant," Wes said finally, looking back at the lobster pots again.

Daphne laughed, delighted. "It does, doesn't it? But you most definitely wouldn't want to cook food in those dye pots."

Huh, so that's what they were for, Wes thought.

"Care for a crash course?"

"Yes, please," Harry said breathlessly, eyes sparkling, while Wes just nodded.

"So, basically, to dye yarn, you have to cook it," Daphne told them with a grin, gesturing toward the lobster pots.

"For a solid color you literally put water in a pot, add your dye, toss in your yarn, stir it all up together, and then heat it up. Or you can bathe it in a steamer if it's just a small amount of yarn that your dyeing," she added, gesturing toward where the steamers stood. "The pots, obviously, hold more.

"Then, once the bath reaches the right temperature, you add in your citric acid to set the color."

"What's the right temperature, or is that a trade secret?" Wes asked, eyeing the burners.

"No, it's not. And it's one hundred and seventy-five degrees."

Well, that was precise enough.

"How do you know how much dye to put in?" Harry asked, looking back at the jars on the wall.

"The depends on what your trying to do. The amount of dye you put in dictates the richness of the color."

That made sense.

"It takes practice to get it right, I'm afraid. Not to mention that different yarns take color differently. Anyway, once it's done being cooked, you drain the water, rinse out the yarn, and hang it up to dry. And that's pretty much it. For a solid, that is.

"Speckled yarns, for instance, are made quite differently. For one thing, you paint it on a tabletop," she gestured to the island with all the measuring cups and droppers on it. "So, basically, you mix your dye up, along with the citric acid, and then you use a dropper to place the color on the yarn where you want it. When you're done, you wrap it up in Saran Wrap then pop it in one of the steamers to cook."

"Why am I thinking it's not actually that easy?" Wes asked her dryly.

"Because it isn't!" she agreed, laughing. "But not to worry. That's why I have helpers for the workshop."

Looking around the studio one last time, Wes let his eyes linger on the baskets full of undyed skeins of yarn that were on display against the far wall. Floor-to-ceiling closets jostled the yarn for space. Through their open doors Wes could see what appeared to be sliding arms that looked like you might hang dish towels on them.

"What are those for?" he asked, pointing toward them.

Daphne turned around to look. "Those are the drying racks. The arms slide out to make it easier to hang the wet yarn on, then they push back in again out of the way when you're done with them."

Clever. The whole place was clever, Wes thought, looking around it again. And expensive. No wonder Grace and Meredith had pooled their resources together.

"Do all dye studio's look like this?" he asked, because he wasn't entirely sure Grace and Meredith could have afforded a set up like this, even going in on one together. Which they hadn't. They'd both had their own studios and, from what Meredith had said, the math didn't quite add up.

"Heavens no. This is more—state of the art—while all you really need is something to cook your yarn in. Even a microwave will do, in a pinch."

Well, that explained that, then.

Wes wasn't sure what he'd been expecting before he'd stepped into Daphne's studio, but this hadn't been it.

"So what do you think?" Daphne asked.

"It's magical," Harry said softly.

"Well, it will be once you've painted your skeins," Daphne said, smiling happily. "I love seeing what my students come up with."

"I bet some of the things are truly terrifying," Wes said dryly.

Daphne laughed again. "I will not lie to a Federal Agent. Occasionally, and only occasionally mind, some of the things created in this room are the stuff nightmares are made of!" She shuddered theatrically.

"In that case, I'm doomed," Harry said, sighing.

"I doubt that, my dear. You have far too much fashion sense to create anything truly horrifying."

Which, naturally, made Harry beam with pleasure.

CHAPTER THIRTEEN

"So spill, who's Dale Clay, besides being one of the local deputies?" Harry asked once they were back in the SUV.

"What makes you think he's anyone important?"

"You did," she said smugly. "You did that *thing*."

He glanced at her sideways. "What *thing*?"

She reached over and patted his cheek. "That thing where you tug on your hair and it gets all messy?"

Oh, *that* thing. He couldn't deny that he did it, either. He tugged on his hair when he was thinking or frustrated. "I'll tell you who he is over lunch, how's that? Because I don't know about you, but I'm starving."

"Fine. But just for keeping secrets from me, I want dessert too," she told him firmly.

Like dessert had ever been in question.

They found the mom-and-pop diner Daphne had recommended, not far from her studio. Wes thought it was a pretty good bet that the food was good too, since he couldn't see Daphne eating somewhere where she might get food poisoning.

They settled into a corner booth and ordered the meatloaf with mashed potatoes, green beans, and gravy. It didn't get much more cliché than that.

"Okay, now about Dale Clay," Harry prodded, keeping her voice down, since it was more than likely someone in the diner would know who they were talking about. "Daphne said he was a deputy sheriff?"

He let her think that through, watching the wheels turning.

"Wait! He was one of the ones at the crime scene, wasn't he?"

"The *first* one on the scene," he told her, nodding.

Her eyes flew open wide. "And he never told you he was dating the murder victim?"

"No, he didn't," Wes agreed. Which could mean only one of two things: he was either worried about his job, if he couldn't be cleared immediately, or he was guilty. "But then neither did Meredith—or Janine. In fact, when I asked Jan if Grace had a boyfriend, she said no."

"That doesn't mean she lied. Maybe she didn't know? Or maybe . . . maybe they'd broken up recently . . . *Oh!*"

Wes nodded. Yeah. Oh. Kind of a big "oh." Big enough to add Dale Clay's name to his suspect list, even if the fact he'd lied by omission hadn't put him on it already.

"Well, it looks like you two were hungry!" their waitress said, beaming at them a short time later. "I only came over to see how you were doing, and you're done already! So how about a piece of pie? We have cherry, peach, apple, blueberry, and coconut cream. With or without homemade vanilla ice cream."

They settled on one piece of blueberry and one piece of peach, so they could share, with ice cream on both of them, of course. And coffee.

"That doesn't mean he killed her though," Harry said once their pie was in front of them.

"Doesn't look good for him either," Wes pointed out. "It's funny though," he went on, rubbing his chin thoughtfully, "but when I asked Meredith if Grace had a boyfriend, she specifically told me no. No, that's not quite right." He frowned, searching his memory. "She said, not right now."

"And she would have known," Harry said excitedly, "which means they *had* broken up, and not long after Daphne first met them!"

Wes nodded. "More than likely. Except, I also specifically asked Meredith if Grace had any recent exes."

"And let me guess, she said 'no' to that too."

"And no to any *angry* exes."

"Curious and curiouser," Harry murmured. "So, which one's the truth?"

"Something I intend to find out, right after I finish off your pie for you," he added dragging her neglected plate closer.

"You know can order another," she said, smiling at him fondly. "It's not like they were very big pieces to begin with."

He stabbed the last peach from her peach pie and considered it. He *had* been torn between the cherry and blueberry, and both pies had been exceptionally good . . .

"Okay, but only if you happen to have a pad of paper in that suitcase you call a purse, so we can review the pitifully few facts I have about the case."

She shot him a dirty look.

"My bad, of course you do," he apologized, hands in the air.

Then he had to bite back a grin as Harry started rummaging around in her purse, pushing aside a pair of spare socks for him, in case his got wet for some reason, a pair of slipper socks for her, that she wore when they were driving long distance, a Kindle, and a knitting project, because god forbid you got caught short with no way to amuse yourself—until she found what she was looking for.

"All right, let's start with the known facts," she told him placing the alarmingly large pad and brand-new mechanical pencil on the table in front of herself.

"You know I couldn't do this without you, right, Watson?" he told her softly.

"Flattery will get you everywhere," she said, blowing a kiss at him. "Now quit stalling, you big lug." Then, in her very worst Bogart, she added, "Give me all the facts, schweetheart."

Taking a sip of his coffee, Wes leaned back, eyes thoughtful as he sifted through everything he'd learned.

"Okay. The facts as I know them," he said finally, nodding his thanks to the waitress as she set down his piece of cherry pie in front of him.

"I know Grace was alive at eight or eight-fifteen, because Janine heard her talking to Meredith on speaker phone.

"I know she was dead by nine because that's when we got to the barn and found her.

"I know Grace and Dale were dating three months ago when they met Daphne.

"And I know that, at the very least, Meredith stood to inherit everything Grace had that pertained to her dye business."

"And?" Harry prodded when he stopped talking.

"And that's it, Red, in a nutshell."

"Well, that's not good," she said, frowning down at her notes.

No, it wasn't.

"There is one more thing," she said thoughtfully.

"What's that, babe?"

She chewed on her lip for a minute, uncertainly, before saying, "Peter, Daphne's PA? He had a thing for Grace. What if he knew Grace and Clay had broken up, but she didn't want any part of him, and he wouldn't take no for an answer?"

That was a lot of what ifs, Wes thought. On the other hand, it was worth looking into, if for no other reason than to cross him off as a suspect.

"Good call," he told her and smiled as she preened, mentally patting herself on the back.

"Where to next?" she asked, as he finished polishing off his cherry pie. "Back to Daphne's to talk to Peter, or to Grace's to talk to Dale, or to Meredith's?"

Twirling his coffee cup first one way and then the other on

its saucer until Harry reached out and stopped him, Wes growled, "I'm thinking, woman."

"No, you were playing," she told him, moving his cup out of reach. "So, who do you want to talk to first?"

Wes stared at his coffee cup thoughtfully. Peter, Dale or Meredith. Peter, Dale . . . or Harry's nosey neighbor . . .

"I think your little old neighbor lady friend," he said, hiding a grin.

"She's not old!" Harry said, predictably, huffing out an exasperated breath.

"No, but if we're lucky she *is* nosey and dying to tell us all kinds of interesting secrets." he said, reaching for the check.

"Too many people keeping secrets," Harry muttered, sliding out of the booth.

"There generally are when someone's been murdered," he told her.

"You know what isn't secret?" she asked, slipping her arm through his as they made their way through the crowded diner.

"How much you love me?"

"Now you're just being ridiculous. I was referring to how good the food in this diner is."

She wasn't lying, Wes thought. It really had been.

"Maybe we can have our wedding reception here," he teased, opening the door for her, then following her outside.

"And how can we do that when you haven't even asked me to marry you?" she asked, grinning up at him. "Besides, wouldn't that be jumping the gun since we're not even 'officially' dating yet?"

She had a point. They'd spent the last year studiously denying it, so their parents wouldn't start bugging them about just that, setting a date, settling down, having babies . . .

But maybe it was time to change their status. Maybe he was finally ready for all that.

"Hey—everyone?" he called out to the people in the parking lot. "This is my girlfriend!"

Which won him a few curious looks, some cat calls, and a few claps.

"There, it's official now," he told her, grinning broadly.

"Idiot!" She smacked his arm before burying her face in his chest and dissolving into giggles.

"What? I thought it was romantic."

"Yes," she howled. "Very. I can hardly wait to see how you plan to propose to me!"

She had a point. He'd have to come up with something spectacularly crazy to top that.

CHAPTER FOURTEEN

"Harriet? Is everything okay? Has something else happened?" Ellen Montrose's worried voice floated out onto her front porch, her anxiety clear, even if Wes hadn't been able to see her hand on her throat.

Harriet? Wes thought, shooting Harry a quick look, because no one in their right mind ever called her that. Not if they didn't want to get smacked in the head with her handbag.

She shot him a little wink, as the woman rushed on. "Oh! You've brought your detective with you! Come in, come in, please," she added, opening her screen door and ushering them through it into her small, tidy living room.

"It's Special Agent," he corrected.

As he followed Harry inside, he distinctly heard her giggle at the woman's misconception, before she covered it with a small ladylike cough.

Ellen stared at him puzzled for a moment, little lines appearing between her eyes before they flew open wide. "You're FBI?"

For a minute, Wes thought she seemed frightened by the thought of it, before her expression changed to one of embarrassment.

"Oh! I'm so sorry," she apologized. "How silly of me. I must have misunderstood Harriet earlier. I thought you were helping the local police find Grace's killer."

"I am," he said. If he hadn't been watching, he might have missed the little tell-tale twitch of her cheek.

Now why would an FBI agent on your doorstep make you anxious unless you were guilty of something? Although it seemed unlikely she was guilty of murder, he thought, taking in her graying blonde hair, cut in a short no-nonsense bob, and her slightly overweight body. Most likely it was something as simple as a small stash of weed, as something nefarious. Especially since her house smelled like patchouli instead of the mothballs he'd thought it would.

"But why? I mean, why would the sheriff call in the FBI?" she rushed on, peering up at him, clearly upset. "Surely it was just a burglary gone wrong or something like that? Not anything the FBI would get involved with."

Behind Ellen's back, Harry was making "you're being big and intimidating" signs, which were kind of hilarious since they included her first reaching up high, then what he thought might have been a gorilla interpretation, followed by her throwing a silent punch into her other hand. And though he knew what she was doing, he had to bite his cheek to keep from laughing out loud.

Besides, it wasn't his fault he took up most of the space in the living room. It was tiny, and he wasn't.

"Normally, no," he agreed sitting down carefully in one of the two dark blue wing-backed chairs Ellen gestured to. "But Sheriff Weaver asked me to assist, since I'm here, so that's what I'm doing. I'm assisting him in his investigation."

"I see," she said, frowning slightly as she settled down into what was obviously "her spot" on the couch. She reached blindly for the knitting she'd obviously been working on before she'd gotten up to answer the door. "I was just telling your dear Harriett earlier that I can't believe someone would kill Grace."

Wes thought he might die from trying not to laugh. His "*dear Harriet*"? Dear god. It didn't help any that Harry was having a mild coughing fit to cover up her fresh spate of giggles.

Evil minx, she might have warned him how weird Ellen Montrose was. Her mannerisms were more suited to someone twice her age and from a long bygone era.

"I mean, poor Gracie. It had to have been an accident. She must have walked in on someone looking for money, and they killed her when she found them."

Unlikely, since they'd left the iPad. But what he asked was, "What makes you think that?" He couldn't imagine what made her think that, other than having watched too many episodes of *Murder She Wrote*. Still, it made a nice change from the *CSI Las Vegas* afficionados he usually ran into.

"Well, it just had to be. I mean who would kill Grace? She was so kind and sweet. Everyone loved her."

Ummmm, West thought. *Someone* hadn't. Or they'd loved her too much. Either one was a possibility.

"So, Ellen, I need to ask you a few questions, if that would be all right?" And even if it wasn't.

"Oh, yes," Ellen exclaimed. "You probably want to know my movements this morning and where I was at the time of the murder," she said with relish.

Wes raise an eyebrow and she blushed.

"I must admit, I do watch those crime shows on TV. So I know how these things go."

Great. Another *CSI Las Vegas* aficionado, after all. Yay.

"Excellent," he said instead, which caused Harry to giggle and cover it up with another little coughing fit again. She knew exactly how he felt about the misinformation those kinds of shows gave as to how agents worked crime scenes and ran investigations.

"Oh dear, I do hope you're not coming down with anything, Harriett," Ellen said, peering at her anxiously.

"No, I'm fine. Probably just something in the air," Harry told her. This time it was Wes who had to cover up a snort with a cough.

Ellen nodded sagely. "Things are in bloom," she agreed.

"Now, where were we? Oh, yes, you were going to ask me about my movements this morning." She paused making a show of thinking, clearly enjoying her moment in the limelight being interrogated by a federal agent.

"Well, I got up at six a.m. as usual. I've always been an early riser. And then I had a cup of tea and an egg and a piece of toast with marmalade—my usual breakfast. Breakfast is an important part of the day. It gets you going," she told them.

Again, Wes had the distinct impression that everything Ellen said and did, from her little "oh"s to the lace doilies on the arms of all her chairs, to her way of speaking, were calculated to make everyone think she was older than she was, for some reason.

"What next?" Ellen said rhetorically, tapping her cheek and humming a little. "Oh, yes. Then I listened to the news to catch the weather because of the dye crawl. Although, I always listen to the weather to know how to dress. It's just so unpredictable, especially this time of year. It can be seventy degrees one day, and then snowing the next, and it would have been awful if it had decided to snow or rain today. Don't you think?"

Wes made little agreeing noises, while Harry snorted into a tissue, clearly enjoying this.

"Then I threw on some old jeans and a T-shirt and hurried over to Grace's, because I'd promised I'd help her finish setting up."

"And that would have been around, when?" Wes asked, hoping to hurry things up.

"About—seven or seven-fifteen. I think. Wait, no, silly me. I flagged down Dale Clay first when I saw him out front."

Wes blinked.

"He was just pulling past the front of the house, and I remember thinking he must have been stopped out there on the road for some reason and had only just started driving again, because he was going really slowly. Anyway, he was just the person I needed to help me move some things out onto the front porch for the Goodwill truck to pick up on Monday."

"Okay," Wes said, filing that away for later, not wanting to get sidetracked right now. "And then you went over to Grace's dye studio."

She nodded. "Yes."

"And how did she seem?"

Ellen bit her lip, staring hard at her knitting for a minute before sighing heavily. "She seemed preoccupied, like she had something weighty on her mind."

"You wouldn't know what that was, would you?"

Again, the hesitation. "No, not really, although I can guess."

Wes made a "go ahead" motion.

"It was something I overheard her say, just as I was leaving, actually. We'd been mixing up the dyes for the workshop, and her head wasn't in it, so I suggested she go finish tidying up in the shop. You know, setting out the gift bags and tissue paper, and hanging up the yarn we'd dyed especially for the dye crawl.

"Anyway, once I was done getting everything ready in the dye studio, I popped into the shop for just a moment to let her know I was running home to shower and change, since it was almost eight-twenty, and she was on the phone."

"Yes?" Wes prodded.

"With Meredith. Meredith Favor."

He nodded.

"She was angry."

"Who was angry? Meredith or Grace?"

"Grace. I couldn't hear Meredith. But Grace was definitely angry."

"If you couldn't hear her, how do you know it was Meredith she was talking to?" he interrupted.

"Because Grace said something like—'there's nothing else to talk about. As soon as the dye crawl's over, we're breaking up Grace & Favors.' I was shocked, of course. I had no idea, but I didn't want to eavesdrop."

My ass, Wes thought.

"So, I just patted her on the arm and whispered I was going home to get ready and then I—left." She hesitated, as if there was something else she wanted to say, hands tightening on her needles, and for just a minute Wes thought she looked angry.

"There was one more thing I heard, when I was leaving." She paused, and if Wes hadn't been looking, he might have missed the way her nostrils flared and her lips compressed right before she said, "I heard Grace say, 'I've had enough, I can't take it anymore!' as I went out the door.

"I'm sorry"—she covered her mouth with her hand, tears gathering in her eyes—"but I can't believe she's gone."

"I'm so sorry," Harry said, moving over to sit beside her on the couch.

"Thank you," Ellen said, patting Harry's hand. "It's just that you don't ever expect someone you know to get murdered."

CHAPTER FIFTEEN

It took Ellen a little while to get ahold of herself again—which, to Wes, seemed to involve a great deal of sniffing and several tissues before she drew herself up and said, "I'm so sorry. I know you have questions."

"I do," Wes agreed, not entirely taken in by her tears and hand wringing. The woman was enjoying this way too much. "Have you known Grace long?" An easy place to start.

"Oh, yes. It must be—four or five years since I met her. It was at one of her shows," she said, warming to the subject. "The poor thing was desperate to pee, and she didn't have anyone to watch her booth, so I offered, because people steal things if you leave your booth empty. We hit it off right from the get-go."

Wes nodded. He knew Janine often "booth sat" at shows for other vendors so they could go pee or grab something to eat or drink.

"So, you were a vendor at the show also?"

Ellen blinked, then giggled. "Oh no, I was a buyer. I bought six skeins of her superwash fingering weight wool that day for a sweater."

Four or five years seemed like a long time to remember a single purchase at some long-ago knit show, but Harry was nodding, so maybe not? He didn't think he'd have remembered, but what did he know?

"I'm guessing that means you weren't neighbors then," Wes stated.

Ellen shook her head. "Not then, no. Grace lived next door, but I lived in Charlottesville. It was one of those little coincidences we discovered when we were in her booth chatting, that we lived just a few towns apart."

"A bonding moment," Harry said, smiling.

"It was," Ellen agreed. "Then I ran into her again at another show a few months later. Same scenario—she needed to pee, and I was there, so I watched her booth again. It was so much fun, just hanging out with her, and we got along famously."

"Did you hang out together here too?" Wes asked, waving vaguely around them.

"No. I had no idea where she lived then. Just 'out in the country,' although I think she knew I lived near the university. I probably mentioned it to her." She shrugged. "We were mostly fiber festival friends for the first few years. Although, we did run into each other every now and again, when she came into town to go to one of the bigger grocery stores or one of the chain hardware stores, the way you do sometimes."

Harry nodded, as if she knew exactly what Ellen meant.

"How did you end up living next door to her?" Wes asked, curious.

"Oh, that was just dumb luck. I started looking at houses because I was ready to get out of town, if you know what I mean? It's great for a while, and then it just wears on you. I wanted to live somewhere quieter and have a garden, not something I could afford in the city, so I started looking farther out. When this one came on the market, I fell in love with it and just gobbled it up."

Something that seemed to happen a lot around here, Wes thought.

"You can imagine my surprise when I found out who my neighbor was! We laughed so hard, and then slowly, one thing led to another, and we just sort of became partners."

Wes blinked. *Partners?* That was the first he'd heard of it. His eyes met Harry's. She seemed equally astonished. So that was not something the general public knew, then. And not something *Meredith* had mentioned, either.

"Partners as in—?" Wes let his question hang in the air. Predictably, she snatched on to it.

"It started small, you know," Ellen said, smiling, "with me just helping Grace dye yarn in her studio and helping out in her booth at shows. I even took packages to the post office for her. I'm an accountant by trade, so you can imagine how stifled my artsy side had been all these years. Working alongside Grace was —exhilarating. A breath of fresh air. And just so much fun too."

Not real partners, then.

"So you went to shows with Grace?" Harry asked ingeniously.

Ellen laughed, excited to share. "Not all of them, but yes, the little ones around here and some of the ones in Maryland and North Carolina too."

"Like Coastal Carolina?" Harry prodded.

An annoyed look flickered across Ellen's face for a moment. An unpleasant memory, Wes thought. "Sadly no. Grace had to go alone. Work," she added, by way of explanation of why she hadn't been there.

"Hmmm. I thought I saw Meredith in their booth when I was there," Harry said, a slight frown on her face, as if she were trying to remember, despite the fact she knew Meredith had been there.

Wes was sure he saw irritation cross Ellen's face, but whether it was at the mention of Meredith or because Harry had been at the show, he didn't know.

"Oh, I didn't mean alone, alone," Ellen said quickly. "Yes, Meredith was there, helping." She added, as if Meredith wasn't, in fact, part of Grace & Favors.

Harry grinned. "Whew. I thought so!"

"And how lucky for you, that you got to go!" Ellen added, all smiles and sweetness again.

"I know. Wes took me," Harry said smugly.

"I know this is hard, but I need you to think back to this morning when you left the dye studio to come home and change," Wes said, taking control of the conversation again. "Did you see anything out of the ordinary? A person or a car that looked out of place?"

Ellen shook her head. "No, not really. I wasn't looking, and I took the path through the hedge anyway, so I wouldn't have seen anyone out on the street. But really, I just went straight out the back door of the studio through the hedge and into my house through my own back door. Just like I always do.

Wes blinked. "The path through the hedge?"

What path?

Ellen laughed. "Well, it's not a proper hedge, just a row of butterfly bushes between our two properties. Grace loved butterflies and planted all kinds of yummy plants for them to eat, and I've always liked them myself."

Wes had guessed as much, judging by the framed pictures of butterflies all over the living-room walls and the two large needlepoint butterfly pillows at either end of the couch.

"Anyway, the path through the hedge? Well, it's more like a *gap* through the hedge. Especially this time of year, when the butterfly bushes aren't in bloom. More like a space, really, about one person wide where a bush had died. We never got around to replacing it."

"Anyway, the only other person I saw was Meredith, but that was a little bit after I got home. Maybe around eight-twenty-five a.m. or so? I was about to hop in the shower, but I was out of soap. I keep the spares in the pantry, so I was in the kitchen, and

I happened to glance out the window. She was in her backyard just walking about."

There was nothing quite like a nosey neighbor. Pity she hadn't seen anyone running out of the back of the barn, too, Wes thought, carding his fingers through his hair. He had just started to give it a tug when he noticed Harry grinning at him.

Fine! Dropping his hand into his lap, he looked back at Ellen and asked, "Do you know of anyone who might have been angry with Grace? A customer, an ex-boyfriend, a current boyfriend?"

"No," Ellen said, shaking her head, but Wes caught the slight fluttering of her pulse in her neck. So she was lying about one of them.

"You're sure?" he pushed.

"Yes. Grace's customers all loved her, and she didn't have a boyfriend." Her voice trailed off like she was thinking about something.

Harry's eyes met Wes's. Her eyebrows rose, and he knew exactly what she was thinking. Ellen had seemed very sure Grace hadn't been seeing anyone.

"Although . . . there was this one young man I saw over at Grace's several times in the past few months. He was tall, with dark hair. I think he was either English or Australian? I can never tell those accents apart. But I do know he drove a—*oh!*"

"Oh?"

"Oh dear. I might have seen the killer's car."

"When?" Wes demanded, his voice harsher than he'd intended. It made the woman flinch a little.

"I—I don't know exactly. But it was after I left the dye studio. Let me think," she tapped her lips. "I got in the shower around eight-thirty, between walking home from the studio and getting clean clothes and everything. Then after my shower, I went and got another cup of coffee in the kitchen and came to sit in the living room to drink it. That's when I noticed a bag of things for Goodwill that somehow hadn't made it out onto the porch.

"And even though I was only in my robe, it wasn't like I expected anyone to be about, so I decided to just go ahead and put it on the porch before I forgot about it again. And that's when I saw the car driving off down the road."

"Can you describe the car, Ellen?" Wes asked.

She nodded, assertively. "Yes. It was a gray Dodge Charger you know like the sheriff's deputies drive? And I know a lot of other people drive them, as well but, it's just that—that young man I was telling you about? The one who was interested in Grace? Well, I think he might drive one too."

CHAPTER SIXTEEN

"Do you believe her?" Harry asked, once they were back in the SUV, the engine rumbling softly as they sat at the end of Ellen's driveway.

Wes huffed out a breath. Eyewitnesses were notorious for getting things wrong. But if she *had* seen a gray Dodge Charger, and if Peter Sutcliff drove one, and if he had a crush on Grace like Daphne had said . . .

"Anything's possible. And it's easy enough to check out."

"And if he does drive a gray Dodge Charger?" Harry pushed.

"Then I'll need to find out where he really was around eight-forty this morning." Assuming it hadn't taken Ellen more time than that to shower because according to Daphne Goshart, Peter Sutcliff had been at her dye studio by nine o'clock.

"And what was with Ellen's kooky old-woman act?" He asked. "She's, what, in her mid-forties?" At the oldest.

Harry giggled, her eyes alight with laughter. "Right?

Honestly, a couple of times there, I thought I was going to wet my pants."

"You could have warned me."

"I could have," Harry agreed. "But where would the fun have been in that?"

With a shake of his head, Wes sighed, his thoughts going elsewhere as he ran his fingers through his hair and gave it a tug. "Yes, I know what I'm doing, woman," he growled. "Don't stop me. I'm thinking."

"I wouldn't dream of it," she said, smirking before lifting a sock she was knitting out of her project bag.

Listening to the rhythmic snick of her needles, Wes felt himself relax.

"Where to now, Sherlock?" she asked after a bit.

"I'm thinking Meredith's," he said finally. "I want to know what was really going on with their partnership and what, if anything, she knows about Grace and Peter." There were other things he wanted answers to, as well. Like why she hadn't told him about Dale Clay.

And he had a whole list of questions for Dale Clay himself.

But Meredith's first, he thought, glancing at the car's digital clock as he pulled out of Ellen's driveway, because he had another reason for needing to be at Meredith's right about, now.

"And," he added with a sly glance sideways at Harry, "correct me if I'm wrong, but I think it's almost time for Meredith's workshop to begin. A workshop my girlfriend very much wants to take."

"Oh!" Harry said, speechless for once.

"What do you think?"

"I think that if you're interrogating Meredith, she can't be running her workshop," she pointed out.

"And you would be correct, my lovely Watson, except for the fact that she already told me Janine was more than capable of handling it. So, guess who's going to be doing just that?"

"Seriously? That's awesome! Janine's going to be thrilled!"

Or go ballistic. Wes thought. The odds were fifty-fifty.

"Did you figure it out yet, Muscles?" Janine asked, by way of a greeting, bouncing up to them just outside Meredith's shop. A bag of paper towels she must have just gotten from the house tucked under one arm.

"No, not yet. But the real question is—why did you tell me Grace wasn't dating anybody?" Wes asked her, glowering just slightly.

"Because she isn't—wasn't. At least, not that I know of? It's not like we were buds, Wes. If you want to know who Grace was or wasn't seeing why don't you ask Meredith—after all they *were* BFF's." The 'duh' was unspoken.

Then, turning to Harry with an eyeroll, she said, "I have no idea what you see in this big lug."

"I find his 'luginess' very attractive," she answered, grinning.

Returning her grin, Janine said, "To each their own."

"Hey, I'm standing right here?" Wes protested.

"Which begs the question—why exactly?" Janine asked him.

"Because, A: I need to speak to Meredith again and, B: Harry is going to take the workshop that you will now be conducting, because of A."

"Oh hell, no!" Janine exclaimed.

"It'll be fine," Harry told her, taking her arm and getting her started toward the studio's front door. "Especially since Meredith told Wes earlier how you were more than ready to take over for her if need be."

"Well, yeah," The teen agreed, preening slightly. "And it's probably not a bad idea, actually," she added thoughtfully. "She's been struggling, trying to be all happy and smiley while knowing Grace is dead. So, yeah, okay. I can do it—if Merry agrees," she added, throwing a look at Wes. "And, I'm glad you'll be in there with me." She gave Harry a quick little hug.

"Oh, she'll agree," Wes told her, his smile all teeth. Which had the teen whirling around and poking a finger into his chest.

"You be nice to Merry, you hear me, Muscles?" She demanded, eyes flashing. "If you're mean to her, I swear, I will take you on myself!"

"Scout's honor," Wes agreed.

"You were probably never even a scout," Janine said sniffly. Not waiting for an answer, she pulled open the door to the shop and stepped inside.

CHAPTER SEVENTEEN

"Did you find out something, is that why you're back?" Meredith asked anxiously, sinking down onto the loveseat and drawing her legs under her.

The orange cats were sprawled out on the couch again, their green eyes daring him to push them aside, so Wes took the lime-green armchair again.

"I did, and yes, that's why I'm here." He let the silence draw out between them for a minute before saying, "Why didn't you tell me Grace and Dale Clay were dating?"

Meredith made a little gasping sound, drawing the attention of one of the cats. "Because they weren't!" she protested. "Not anymore." She shook her head, then sunk into herself, shoulders hunching, arms wrapping around her middle, rocking just a little.

A classic case of shutting down, Wes knew—a symptom of

both not wanting to say anything else and desperately needing to.

He wracked his brain for how Fountain would have handled it, because this was exactly where his partner would have stepped in and taken over to prevent Wes from using intimidation to keep their witness talking.

One of the cats raised its head, threw Wes a filthy look, then leaped from the couch to the love seat and snuggled up against Meredith. The other one yawned first, showing Wes all its fangs, before joining its litter mate.

"Slow and easy," he could hear Fountain's voice. "Make a connection. Be nice. Be sympathetic. Find something else to ask them. Something they'll grab on to. Win their confidence, so you can gently lead them back to what it is they aren't telling you."

Easy for him to say, he was a trained psychiatrist.

But Wes was a trained investigator. Trained to *notice* things. Like the spray of tattooed butterflies he could see where Meredith's yoga pants had ridden up on her calves when she'd curled up.

From where he was sitting, they looked exactly like the ones he'd seen on Grace.

It was worth a shot.

"Tell me about the butterflies."

Her head shot up. "The *what?*"

He gestured toward them. "The tattoos."

"Oh," a sad smile slipped across her face.

Picking up one of the cats, she settled it onto her lap before saying, "We got them together, in college, as a joke, really. Or at least that's how it started." She rubbed her fingers across one on her calf. The first one they'd gotten, Wes suspected, its wings half opened, as if it were just getting ready to fly.

"The ugly caterpillars, that's how we saw ourselves, learning to spread our wings and becoming beautiful butterflies in the process. Or that was what they were supposed to represent, anyway.

"It was a metaphor, really, for doing what *we* wanted, instead of what was expected of us. Our parents were old fashioned, you now? They expected us to go to college and get our MRS degrees, because in their minds, that's what women did."

Their what? He didn't know that one.

At his puzzled look she explained, "MRS—as in, becoming someone's wife."

Mrs.—now he got it.

"That's all college was to them," she went on, "a place to find suitable men to marry so we'd always be looked after. Like we weren't *capable* of doing anything, except for having babies and keeping house. So, majoring in art was fine. What we weren't supposed to do was graduate and then run off to start yarn-dyeing businesses and skip getting married."

"Which is what you did, instead." Their parents must have loved that.

She nodded. "The butterflies were the start of the 'great rebellion,' because, according to our parents, who would want to marry a tattooed woman?" She gave a little laugh. "It was step one in the great plan.

"It started out innocently enough. Just a small one," she tapped a tiny butterfly at the side of her knee, "and then it took off from there." She smiled down at the swirling spiral.

"We got them to commemorate milestone events. An art project that turned out well, a summer internship with someone we admired. We celebrated each other's wins, getting the same tattoos because that's what best friends do." Her voice hitched, breaking off. "And we were. Best friends, since grade school."

"Did you grow up here?"

She sniffed, tears hovering on her eyelids. "No. We grew up in Roanoke, so going to UVA wasn't that far from home, but it was still far enough away to be out from under their thumbs, you know?"

Wes nodded. He hadn't wandered far away either. Just far enough.

"When we graduated, Grace didn't want to leave. She loved it here. But I wanted to move to California—spread my wings. So I did." She stroked a blue butterfly near her ankle. "We got this one to commemorate me flying away. It hurt like hell—the tattoo not the leaving," she clarified. "Of course, I missed Grace like crazy, but I needed to get away to find out who I was."

"So, you left."

She nodded. "Yeah. And it was good, for a while. Until it wasn't."

"What happened?"

"The usual. I met Mr. Right, who turned out to be Mr.

Wrong. At least I found out he was cheating on me before the wedding." Her lip quivered. "Grace convinced me to come back home. To come here. And as luck would have it, this house was for sale. It seemed like fate. BFF's forever." A tear trickled down her cheek, and she let it fall. Her fingers carded through the cat's fur furiously. It wriggled and made a plaintive 'meow,' and her hand stilled before she patted it gently.

"But that's not what happened. Something went wrong, didn't it?" he prodded.

She shook her head. "No. Something went right—except —*shit!*"

Wes let the silence lengthen. He had a feeling they were finally circling back to what Meredith hadn't told him.

She licked her lips and started her story somewhere different than he'd been expecting.

"Grace started dating this guy a few months ago. She was really into him, and I was excited for her. Just 'cause my love life sucked didn't mean hers had to as well. But we were crazy busy at the time. Running from one show to another, then beetling home to fall in the dye pots so we could race off to another show. It seems crazy now, looking back on it, but I only met him about a month ago.

"I never meant for it to happen. Neither of us did. But there was this—attraction—from the moment we met. Like electricity arcing between us."

"Between you and Dale Clay, Grace's boyfriend?" He had not seen that coming.

Her shoulders fell. "Yes." Her voice was barely a whisper.

"And she found out you two were cheating on her?"

Meredith's head shot up. "No! I'd never—not after what had happened to me. We never acted on it, not while they were still together. I couldn't. I *wouldn't*. She was my *best friend*." A sob caught in her throat.

"It was awful, trying to pretend I didn't want him, that we weren't attracted to each other, and she was oblivious."

"What happened?"

Meredith closed her eyes as a tear trickled down her cheek. "About two weeks ago, Dale just told her." She turned grief-filled eyes on Wes. "I didn't know until Grace came storming over here."

She took a shaky breath, pulling the cat up to her chest. "It was horrible. She accused me of stealing him, and I hadn't! I hadn't done anything. I would never have hurt her. Never. And she was so hurt. So *angry*. She wanted to break up Grace & Favors and go our own separate ways. She wanted nothing else to do with me.

"I didn't want to lose her, Agent Smith. I didn't want Dale to come between us, but I didn't know how to fix it. I tried talking to her, but she wouldn't talk to me about it.

"I thought, I thought maybe, after the dye crawl, after she'd calmed down a bit, that given a little distance, she'd realize he wasn't 'the one,' and that maybe then we could patch things up. Make things right between us again.

"If he'd just broken up with her, let it lie for a little bit, and then asked me out—not told her he was dumping her for me, none of this would have happened! She probably would have thought it was funny—it happened all the time to us in college . . .

"She was my best friend for twenty-five years, Agent Smith, and I let a guy come between us. Now she's dead, and I can't ever make it up to her. I don't know if I can even bear to look at him again."

Death had a way of doing that. Leaving things broken with no way to go back and fix them.

"Do you know a Peter Sutcliff?"

She stared at him, confused, her thoughts and misery elsewhere. "I—no?"

"Tall, dark hair, works for Daphne Goshart as her PA."

"I—I didn't know his last name."

"Know a lot of Peter's, do you?" He let a little steel seep into his voice, the time for being nice over. She flinched, pulling into herself and ducking her head. The cat in her lap glared at him and lashed its tail.

"Tell me about him," he pushed.

"He had a thing for Grace," she admitted. "But she wasn't interested because she had—Dale." Her voice broke on his name. Then she sniffed, a watery smile on her lips. "We laughed about it. How he was her 'boyfriend in waiting,' because he kept coming by anyway."

"And after? Once they'd broken up, was he still hanging around?"

She nodded. "I think so, yes. I saw his car there a few times when I went by to drop things off at the barn. But I think it was just wishful thinking on his part. She wasn't ready to move on. If he'd waited, I think, given it some time, they might have been good together."

He left her with her cats and her grief, closing the front door quietly behind himself, thinking how maybe Peter hadn't been so willing to wait, after all.

CHAPTER EIGHTEEN

Pausing outside Meredith's front door, Wes sifted through the things she'd told him, undecided as to how truthful she'd been.

Grief was a funny thing.

He'd met plenty of killers who'd grieved for the person they'd killed because they were dead, but not because they'd killed them.

He'd met others who had grieved for the killing itself, but not for the person they'd killed. And a handful who'd grieved for both.

And while he didn't think it was likely Meredith had murdered Grace, he wasn't quite ready to cross her name off his pitifully small list of suspects just yet, because she'd had something to gain besides a boyfriend. And the truth, he knew, was always stranger than fiction.

Wes got into his SUV and pointed its nose back down Meredith's driveway. He needed to talk to Dale Clay, and he had plenty of time before he needed to pick up Harry from the work-shop. Time enough, he thought, to also swing back by Daphne's and talk to her PA about where he'd really been that morning too.

If Ellen Montrose was right and the car she'd seen had been his, then that put him near the scene of the crime right about the time Grace had been murdered.

"Sheriff? If I could grab you and Deputy Clay for a minute," Wes asked, coming up beside the two men where they stood just off to the side of the barn, watching the CSIs work their magic on the blood spatter inside. "In private," he added, letting a little gravel drift into his words.

Clay's head whipped around, eyes opening wide, before he could stop himself. The sheriff studied Wes's face carefully a moment before nodding. "Sure thing. How about up at the house again?"

That worked for Wes.

"Hey, Jeb, keep an eye on things down here. We're going up to the house," Weaver called out to him. "And make sure no one disturbs us. Unless they have to," he tacked on, dryly.

Jeb nodded. "Got it." His eyes never left whatever he was watching; he was clearly fascinated by what he was seeing. And Wes remembered the sheriff saying how Clay was the only deputy he currently had on staff who had crime-scene experience.

Glancing back at Jeb, with his obvious interest and lack of queasiness, Wes thought he'd make an excellent investigator with a little training.

"Not sure how much longer we're going to be able to keep the lid on this thing," Weaver confided as they made their way into the house. "Folks are starting to clog up the phone lines asking what the devil's going on out here."

"I don't think you're going to have to keep them guessing too much longer," Wes told him. That definitely grabbed the sheriff's attention.

"You got a suspect, then?"

"Several," Wes told him, pouring himself a cup of coffee from what looked like a fresh pot someone had made recently. "But right now, I have a few questions for Deputy Clay that need answering."

That was when Wes discovered he never wanted to play poker with Sheriff Weaver. The man's expression didn't change one bit. He simply nodded and turned his gaze on Clay, pointing at a chair, and said, "Sit."

Wes took his time pulling his own chair out from the small kitchen table and sitting down on it. He waited politely for the sheriff to finish fixing his own cup of coffee, studying Clay all the while. The man's gaze flickered up to his briefly, before they skittered away again.

"So, Dale," Wes said, once they were all situated. He shifted his weight on the spindle-legged kitchen chair and hoped it would stand up to his weight when it creaked ominously beneath him. "When were you going to tell me you were dating Grace Harper?"

For a heartbeat, the room was dead silent. Then the front legs on the chair Sheriff Weaver had tipped back slammed down, hitting the ground with a sound like a thunderclap.

"What the hell?" he roared, making Clay flinch.

"I," he started. "We—" Then he came to a stuttering halt beneath the sheriff's furious gaze.

"You *what?* Spit. It. Out." Weaver growled.

"We weren't. Dating, I mean. *Shit.*" Clay closed his eyes for a moment, composing himself. When he opened them again, he went on more calmly. "We were, but we broke up weeks ago."

"Define weeks," Weaver demanded.

Clay's Adam's apple bobbed as he swallowed hard.

"Two. Two weeks. We broke up two weeks ago."

"And you didn't think that was something we needed to know? That it was relevant?" the sheriff demanded.

Meeting the sheriff's eyes, he said, "I knew it would make me a suspect."

Got that right, Wes thought. But what he said was, "So, what happened, Dale?" in as kindly a voice as he could manage, even though he already knew the answer. He was trying to play the good cop to Weaver's bad one. Not a role he played often or particularly well.

Clay looked away, rubbing his jaw. "I met someone else."

The sheriff threw him a disgusted look. "Grace caught you cheating, did she? Threw you out, and you got angry? So you thought you'd come back and teach her a lesson? Show her who was boss?" Weaver demanded, voice like granite.

"No! I didn't! I'd never hurt Grace." The sheriff's eyes narrowed, and Wes knew he'd heard that one before. "And I'm the one who broke it off, anyway," Dale added, "before I ever went out with Merry."

"Meredith Favor?" the sheriff asked, plainly shocked. "Lovely," he muttered under his breath.

"How did she take it? Grace?" Wes asked, keeping his voice neutral. Curious as to Clay's take on it.

Clay sighed. "Not well. She was angry." He shook his head. "I really screwed things up. I shouldn't have told her I wanted to break up with her so I could date Meredith instead."

Ya think?

Weaver shook his head as he shot Wes a look.

"I just didn't think it was that big of a deal. People change their minds all the time, right? And we'd only been dating a few months."

"Define a few months," Weaver said, voice less gruff.

Clay shrugged. "Three or four, maybe?"

"But she, what, thought it was going to be forever?" Weaver asked, his voice kinder now that it appeared Clay's only crime had been one of bad judgement.

Now, if Grace had killed Clay that would have been another story. But apart from not telling them the truth to begin with, the only other thing Clay seemed to be guilty of was dumping Grace for Meredith.

Clay shrugged, shoulders sagging in relief at not being yelled at by his boss anymore. "Maybe? But I don't know why. It wasn't like I'd moved in with her or anything."

"It happens," Weaver said, as if he were talking from experience.

"And then she went and threatened to break up Grace & Favors over it," he exclaimed, clearly outraged because of it. "Why would she do that? Why would she punish Merry for something that I did?" he demanded, his anger rising along with his voice at every word.

Which kept him on the suspect list as far as Wes was concerned.

CHAPTER NINETEEN

Well, that hadn't turned out quite how he'd expected, Wes thought, as the sheriff and Clay walked ahead of him back toward the barn. The sheriff's hand on Clay's shoulder like he was consoling him.

The whole "you're not a suspect thing" had ruffled Wes's feathers a bit, until Weaver had turned and caught his eye, giving Wes a nearly imperceptible nod. So, he hadn't completely bought into Clay's innocence. Not after his little outburst over Grace's threat to Meredith.

As he'd noted before, Sheriff Weaver was no country bumpkin. He knew exactly what he was doing following up his bull in a china shop routine with sympathy and a metaphorical shoulder to vent on. As far as Wes could tell, he had suckered the young deputy in completely.

If it turned out Clay was innocent, he didn't have any bridges to mend, and if he wasn't, Wes shook his head, grateful that the fallout from that scenario wouldn't be his problem.

Which reminded him.

"Clay? Where were you this morning between eight-fifteen and eight-forty-five? I forgot to ask," he added, as both the deputy and sheriff stopped on the walkway to look back at him.

He'd purposefully kept his voice light as if he thought it was a stupid, although necessary, question.

Clay nodded, as if he completely understood. "I was—uh, on patrol in the general area," he answered, his eyes not quite meeting Wes's until he added, "which is why I responded to the 9-1-1 call so quickly."

"Thanks," Wes answered, keeping his smile relaxed and friendly, even though the man had lied to him. So instead of being on patrol, where were you really? Wes thought. Fleeing the scene in your patrol car? Was Clay who Ellen had seen driving away? Or had he been somewhere else entirely? Something tugged at his memory. Something Meredith had said maybe? Or hadn't said.

Running his fingers through his hair, he tugged on it unconsciously, making it stand up like the bristles on an angry hedgehog. Damn it, he couldn't remember, but it would come to him. Eventually. For now, he'd go talk to the elusive Peter Sutcliff and see what lies *he* wanted to tell.

"Back again? Although you seem to have lost your girlfriend,"

Daphne said, slipping up beside him as Wes paused just inside the doorway of her shop.

"She's at Meredith Favor's workshop."

Daphne gave a pleased smile. "Good, then she'll have already learned the basics before she does mine. But you're not here to chat, I'd wager."

"No. I really need a quick word with your staff."

"Right then," she nodded, "let me grab Adam and China first —if you can see them together?"

He nodded.

"Good. I won't be a minute, they're in the studio setting out more workstations, since we had a few people just phone in to sign up for the workshop."

"I can talk to them in there. I've only got a few questions, and that way they can keep on working."

"Perfect. Let me know when you're done, and I'll extricate Peter from his fan club," she said wryly, indicating the gaggle of women encircling him as he helped them with their purchases. "Happens every time," she said fondly. "Come on, then. I'll just introduce you to Adam and China, so they don't freak out. They don't know anything's happened beside an 'incident.' I didn't want to tell them."

"What about Peter? Does he know what happened to Grace?"

"No, although for a different reason."

"Because he was—quite taken with her?" he offered, dredging up the exact words she'd used earlier.

Daphne nodded. "Yes. I didn't see any need to tell them, and I got the impression you wanted to keep it fairly quiet. Besides, on a purely selfish level, I need all their heads in the game, or the workshop will be a shambles."

Excellent. But what he told her was, "I won't be telling them either."

"Adam, China? This is Wes Smith. He has a few questions for you to help out in the police inquiry about the incident over at Grace Harper's this morning."

And Wes had to bite back a smile at how very British she sounded. He'd never heard anyone use the term 'police inquiry' before, except in the British murder mysteries that Harry loved to watch on TV.

"And I'll leave you to it," she said, disappearing back out through the doorway.

The two college students looked at him curiously. "Yeah, sure," they said almost simultaneously, not in the least bit nervous about being questioned by "the police."

The young man, Adam, was fairly short, with purple hair and thick black-rimmed glasses. The edges of what Wes thought might be tattooed full sleeves just visible where the cuffs of his shirt had been pushed up. The girl, China, on the other hand, was a willowy blonde with short, spiked hair, large brown eyes and several eyebrow piercings.

"This won't take long," Wes assured them. "I'd just like to know where you were between eight and nine this morning."

"We were in the shop, finishing up the yarn display," China said briskly. No hesitation.

Adam nodded. "Yeah, we hadn't got all the fingering weight hung up yet, since it wasn't dry until this morning."

And Wes couldn't help but feel a little bit smug since he knew what fingering weight yarn was. The stuff Harry knit socks and shawls out of.

"And you were both together the whole time? Neither one of you left for anything?"

"I popped out to go to the loo," China said in her best parody of an English accent. Wes couldn't help but grin, while Adam rolled his eyes and pushed her.

"Be serious. He's a copper!" he told her in his own fake accent that was truly terrible.

"Yeah, don't take up acting," she told him. "That was horrible."

"Says you."

"Yeah, says me."

"What about Daphne? Do you know where she was?" Wes interrupted.

"Ummm. She and Peter came in here to the studio after breakfast, right?" China said, looking at Adam.

"Yeah," he nodded. "Then Daphne went back upstairs to rest for a bit before the dye crawl started."

"Could she have left without you seeing her go?"

Adam was already shaking his head, "no."

"The stairs are right off the side of the shop," he said, which

Wes had already known, "and there's no other way out." Which he hadn't known.

But the dye studio most definitely had another way out, because he was looking at it. A white-painted door set into the wall directly opposite him.

"And Peter? Did he stay in the studio?"

This time, it was China who shook her head.

"No, he went out right after he checked in on us."

"And you know that how?" Wes asked, keeping his voice calm and level even as a frisson of excitement slithered down his back.

She grinned. "Because he was grumbling about having to park his precious car out on the road when he got back, even though it wasn't quite nine o'clock yet. Apparently, the parking area out front was already so packed, that some idiot had blocked the driveway that leads around back."

"Do you know what kind of car he drives?"

"Yeah," Adam answered, with just a hint of jealousy, "a gray Dodge Charger with all the bells and whistles."

"You wouldn't happen to know about what time he left, do you?" Wes asked casually.

"Hmmmmm. We all came down from breakfast, about eight or a little before that, and he and Daphne went into the studio almost right away. They couldn't have been in there more than five minutes maybe?" Adam looked at China for confirmation.

"Sounds about right. He left a few minutes later, after Daphne went back upstairs."

So, if he'd left at eight-ten, say, that would have put him at Grace's at around eight-twenty-five. That would have given him plenty of time to see Grace, get into an argument, kill her, and be back on the road just in time for Ellen Montrose to have seen him after her shower.

"Just one more question. Do you know what he was wearing when he left here this morning?" Wes asked them.

They exchanged a look.

"Noooo," China told him. "But he was wearing blue jeans and a white dress shirt at breakfast if that helps any?"

"Thank you," Wes told them, and he couldn't help it if there was just the hint of a purr in his voice, because when he and Harry had been at Daphne's shop earlier, Peter Sutcliff had been wearing *black* jeans, with a *blue* dress shirt and a brightly knitted fair isle vest over it.

"So, Peter," Wes said a short time later, the smile on his face not particularly friendly. "Where were you between let's say eight and nine this morning?"

They were standing in the little hallway just behind the shop that led upstairs, so Peter could be close by if Daphne needed him.

"Um," he frowned, eyes staring over Wes's shoulder before his face lightened. Looking back at Wes, he said, "I was in the studio with Daphne. Well, not for all of it," he corrected. "We went in there after breakfast to make sure we had enough of everything set out for the workshop. And then," he paused, "then Daphne went upstairs, maybe five minutes later? I looked in on Adam and China to make sure things were going smoothly with them, and then I left out the back of the studio to go for a drive before the dye crawl began."

"Which was about when?"

He rubbed his chin. "I dunno. Maybe eight o'five? It couldn't have been much later, maybe a little earlier."

"And where did you go?"

He gave a little laugh, "You're going to think this is foolish, but I went over to Grace Harper's."

Okaaay. He hadn't expected the man to admit it.

"I've had a bit of a crush on her ever since I met her, but she had a boyfriend, so I was out of luck. Until a few weeks ago, that is. They broke up, so I've been lending her my shoulder to cry on."

"And about when did you get to Grace's?"

"Ummmm. About eight-fifteen, maybe?"

"And did you see her?"

Peter snorted out an annoyed breath. "No. Her ex's car was up by the house, and I didn't want to get in the middle of whatever was going on up there."

Wes blinked. Clay had been there?

"So, I drove round for a bit, thinking I'd pop in after he left. Make sure she was okay. But when I went by the house again a little bit later, he was parked at the *end* of her driveway."

"And about what time was that?"

"Um. eight-thirty?"

"And then what?"

"And then I left. I couldn't hang about any longer since I needed to get back here and change. I'd spilled some dye on my jeans and shirt when I was moving it around earlier and I couldn't very well show up at the dye crawl with red splotches all over me."

Red splotches. Really?

"And then of course, when I got back it was only to find someone had blocked the drive that leads around back so I had to park out on the road, then sort of slide past all the people waiting to get in so they didn't see me. I looked like I'd bathed in blood and I didn't want to scare anybody."

Now there was an interesting choice of words.

"Anyway, I just barely had time to toss my clothes on the floor and put on clean ones and make it to the shop in time for it to open."

Wes couldn't decide if the man was so arrogant that he wouldn't be caught that for the most part he'd told the truth, or if he was actually innocent and had nothing to hide in telling it.

"Was there anything else? It's getting a little loud out there," he said apologetically, "and I think I need to get back out to help.

"Just one last thing. Where do you live?" Wes asked. Something he'd need to know for the search warrant he was hoping the sheriff could get for the man's red splotched clothes. It would be easy enough to tell if it was in fact dye, or if it was blood.

"Oh, up at the house with Daphne and her husband. There's

a mother-in-law suite in the basement. God that sounds terrible. It's got massive windows and leads out onto a little terrace type thing."

"A daylight basement?"

Sutcliff snapped his fingers. "Yes! Exactly. I never remember what the Realtor called it. But it made this place even more attractive when we looked at it.

"I have my own little cottage in Little Hibblethwaite, but I'd have had to rent something here, in town, most likely if there hadn't been a separate place for me to stay, and that would have been a complete waste of time, me having to drive back and forth every day."

"Not to mention the fact that both Mrs. *and* Mr. Goshart are workaholics, so this way at least I can make sure they take breaks and eat. And speaking of breaks, I should really get back out there, now – if you're done with me?" He asked; eyebrows raised in question.

"Yes, for now," Wes agreed. Until he could get a warrant so someone could look at the man's clothing, at least.

CHAPTER TWENTY

If he hadn't known better, Wes would have thought he'd just stepped into a meth lab instead of a dye studio.

Or a meth lab that had run headlong into a paintball event, he amended taking in the kaleidoscope of colors splattered across every available surface of Meredith Favor's studio.

While Daphne Goshart's had been meticulously thought out and planned, with no expense spared when it had come to its contents, Meredith Favors' looked like it had been cobbled together over time as money allowed. Which, he was pretty sure, was exactly what had happened as he looked around.

A pair of battered 36" stainless steel sinks stood against the back wall, splashed in blues and reds and greens and a muddy brown mixture Wes thought might be the result of where multiple colors had run together, because he couldn't imagine anyone having chosen to dye something that particular color.

Five-gallon buckets, the kind you mixed paint in and that

had been white at one point, were crammed into the sinks or piled underneath them. Each one now stained in a mind-boggling mixture of turquoise and fuchsia, grays and yellows, greens and purples over a base of muddy brown.

Three-liter measuring cups sat stacked haphazardly on sawhorse tables in the center of the room, along with plastic gallon containers, dusted in primary colored granules.

Stirring sticks and eyedroppers both used and unused littered the tables' surfaces or had rolled onto the floor beneath them.

Along the right-hand wall, four commercial-grade food steamers that had seen better days, sat on a long stainless-steel table, their lids akimbo, dirty water clearly visible inside them. Wes thought they looked like they might have come from some now defunct buffet-style restaurant.

A row of gas burners that looked suspiciously like old campfire stoves, sat under the steamers, their snake-like connectors curling down to the propane tanks they were connected to. More propane tanks lay strewn haphazardly beneath the steamer table, empty, Wes fervently hoped. A lone microwave stood at the end of the counter next to a stack of paper towels.

Looking around the abused and battered room, Wes wondered what the studio had looked like before it had been mauled by the group of overly enthusiastic, novice dyers who were now standing together in small groups of both men and women in front of the tall cabinets that housed the drying racks.

Their excited chatter filled the air as they peered at the skeins of yarn inside them, dyed every color imaginable.

To Wes, they looked like mad scientists.

Blue-paper shower caps covered their hair, while goggles either hung around their necks or still covered their eyes. The matching blue-paper smocks that covered their clothing were now splashed and splattered with dye. Even their shoes had paper booties, like the CSIs wore, which, Wes thought, had been a really smart idea.

And then his eyes darted back to their smocks, to the splashes and splatters that covered them, before he looked back at the drying skeins of yarn again.

Some sported speckles and spots, but there were no splashes on any of them. But in his mind's eye, Wes could clearly picture the yarn hanging in Grace's barn, splattered and splashed, much like the yarn Ellen had been knitting with when he'd interviewed her.

"Janine," he called out, urgently beckoning her over. "The yarn with the speckles on them?"

"Yeah? What about them?"

"Would you ever make something that kind of looked like that but was more splattered than speckled and with splashes of color over them, too, like the splashes on everyone's smocks?"

She glanced around the room frowning. "No, not like that. Not exactly." Taking his arm, she guided him through the closed doors into the shop area side of Meredith's studio.

"See these skeins here? They're speckled and *painted*," she said, showing him some skeins with the familiar spotted dots on them but with very meticulously painted areas of solid color. Not the haphazard splashes that had been at Grace's.

"And this is what it looks like, all wound up," she added, reaching behind the counter. Wes took the caked yarn from her. Ellen's yarn had looked a lot like this, he thought. But the skeins on the wall hadn't looked like the one Janine had just shown him at all.

Looking back through the open doors into the dye studio, Wes's eyes narrowed as he took in the stained buckets again. What if what he'd thought was blood hadn't been blood, after all?

"Why?" Janine asked.

"Because I think whoever killed Grace splashed a bucket of red dye across the yarn in her shop after they killed her."

"Why? Why would anyone do that? Wasn't it enough to kill her?" Janine demanded. "Who would ruin perfectly good yarn too?"

Someone who was very, very angry, Wes thought.

"Speaking of ruining perfectly good yarn, I need to go help those people over there," she added, before darting back into the studio to help a couple who were trying to hang some truly hideously dyed yarn over one of the drying racks.

Wes could only hope, as he followed her back into the studio, that Harry's first foray into the dye pots had gone better.

And speaking of Harry, he had to bite back a laugh when he caught sight of her. Her smock was completely covered in brightly colored splotches. Lifting his phone, he got off a few pictures before she caught sight of him and bounced over, eyes shining brightly.

"Oh my god, Wes, I had so much fun! Wait until you see what I made." Grabbing his arm, she pulled him through the mayhem to where the yarn was hanging inside the drying cupboards. "Look!" she declared, proudly waving an arm at the sodden mess inside.

He obediently looked, trying hard not to laugh, but he couldn't quite help the snort that escaped him. Harry had liberally spotted her yarn with every color of the rainbow and a few Wes was sure might have been her own creation.

"Beast," she said, smacking his arm, even though she was grinning.

"N—n—no," he stuttered, trying hard not to laugh out loud. "I love it," he lied.

"Good," she beamed, a twinkle in her eye, "because I'm totally knitting you a pair of socks with it."

Oh, hell no, he thought. She dissolved into giggles.

"God, I wish you could have seen your face just now! But, no worries, this yarn is mine!" she said, grinning at it proudly. "Now, *this* one," she added pointing at a skein dyed various shades of blue, "is for you."

"And it's lovely," he told her, relieved. "Thank you, because as much as I love you, there is no way in hell I would have worn anything made out of that," he added, pointing at the rainbow-speckled yarn she'd created.

He didn't have anything against rainbows, but that yarn was something he would not have been caught dead wearing. "But it's going to look lovely on you," he added quickly.

"Good save," she said patting his cheek. "And you're right. It is going to look lovely on me," she beamed, admiring it again.

Looking around, he sighed. Damn. "I'm sorry I missed this," he told her. "I was looking forward to playing in the dye pots with you."

"Oh babe," she said, looking stricken.

"Hey, it's all right, Red," he reassured her. "I'll get the chance to create something truly knit worthy later today when we go to Daphne's."

"And I will be delighted to knit it into something for you," she answered, giving him a little kiss on the cheek. "Now, give me a minute to get rid of all this stuff," she said, gesturing to her smock and booties, "and then I want to hear what you've been up to while I was playing."

CHAPTER TWENTY-ONE

"So, spill, what did you sleuth while I was busy?" Harry asked, once they were back in the SUV.

Wes slid her a sidelong glance, a grin dancing across his lips. "I'm not sure that's actually a verb," he told her.

"Don't be ridiculous. Of course it is. Now spill."

"I have a better idea," Wes told her, starting the SUV and guiding it out onto the street. "Why don't I wait until I can tell both you and Sheriff Weaver, together?"

Harry gave him a frowny face. "Meanie."

"Very," he agreed.

"Why can't I come?" Dale Clay objected.

Wes had quite pointedly asked only the sheriff to come up to the house with them, an omission which Weaver noted with a sharp look.

"Shit, you still think I might have done it! What the—"

"You know why you can't come. You're too close to the case," Weaver interjected smoothly, trying to soothe his deputy's ruffled feathers. Wes was relatively certain that despite that being true, Weaver knew that wasn't the reason Wes wanted to exclude him.

"And besides, I need you down here at the barn," the sheriff added.

"To do what? Watch the CSIs put things in baggies?"

"Exactly," Weaver agreed calmly.

"Just great! I'm not welcome, but his girlfriend is?" Clay sneered, storming off to the other side of the parking area.

"He has a point," Weaver said, as they made their way into the kitchen, fussed with drinks, and then sat down at the small kitchen table. "Though I'm assuming there's a good reason you wanted Harry sitting in on this but not Clay? His closeness to the case notwithstanding."

Wes chose his words carefully before answering. "I have three possible suspects, and Harry isn't one of them. But what she is, is very good at seeing things that I sometimes miss."

"I take it this isn't your first murder then?" Weaver asked her.

Keeping it short and sweet, Harry answered, "No, it isn't."

The sheriff nodded, then sighed. "All right, let's hear what you've got so far that makes you still think Clay may have done it."

When Wes didn't answer right away, Harry stepped in.

"Why don't we take it in order, so things don't get left out or muddled up, jumping all over the place?" she said for Weaver's benefit, since she already knew Wes would start at the beginning and take it from there.

Then, reaching into her handbag, she pulled out her pad and pencil again and set them on the table in front of her. As the sheriff watched curiously, she pulled loose four pages, set them on the table in front of her and wrote: "Suspect #1," "Suspect #2," "Suspect #3," and "Grace Harper," one each across the top of each sheet.

Weaver nodded then.

"Portable white board," she told him with a little smirk.

Looking back at Wes, Weaver said, "Looks like we're ready, then. I'm all ears."

"We have a time of death yet?" Wes asked instead.

Pulling a small notebook out from a jacket pocket, Weaver flipped through it until he found the page he was looking for. "Most likely between eight and eight-forty-five, since you called it in at nine o'one. The coroner didn't think she'd been dead very long when you found her."

"We can narrow it down further," Harry told him, writing "Time of Death" on Grace's paper, then adding, "phone call" under it.

The sheriff raised an eyebrow, then looked up at Wes when he took over the narrative.

"According to both Janine Cavanaugh, who you heard tell us, and Meredith Favor, who told me in her interview later, Grace called Meredith a little after eight o'clock this morning. Their neighbor, Ellen Montrose, volunteered that Grace was on the phone around eight-twenty, when I interviewed *her*."

The sheriff nodded, "Well, that certainly confirms what the girl told us, and it narrows things down considerably. Which brings us back around to your suspects."

"I probably do this a little differently than you're used to," Wes told him. "Instead of working suspect to suspect, I like to work across motive, alibis, and means for everyone at the same time."

Weaver leaned back in his chair and made a "go ahead" gesture. "Sounds interesting. Something new the FBI's doing?"

Wes grinned. "No, it's more of a 'Harry and me' thing," he admitted, "but it works well for us." Then, looking over at Harry, he said, "Meredith Favor."

Harry added her name to the top of the first page under "Suspect #1."

"Motive," Wes continued. "By her own admission, she stood to gain Grace's entire inventory of yarn, dyes, and everything else pertaining to Grace & Favors." To Weaver he added, "Apparently, there's a signed statement outlining their agreement. I'd like to get a copy to see if it extended to any bank accounts, her house, or anything else, and if she also had a will."

The sheriff gave a short, sharp nod, digging a pencil end out of a different pocket. "She didn't happen to tell you the name of their attorney, did she?"

Wes nodded. "Freeman, Greene, and Burke."

Weaver wrote it down, his handwriting small and cramped. "I'll have someone nose around and see if there were any life-insurance policies, while we're at it, too."

Wes nodded. While Meredith's grief had been overwhelming, crippling, and genuine, he'd seen that kind of grief before. Not just when a loved one had been inexplicably murdered, but when the suspect had killed a person they loved in a moment of rage or madness over something that, in the end, they regretted heart and soul.

"All right, who's next?" Weaver queried.

"Dale Clay," Wes said evenly, watching as Harry added his name to the top of the next sheet of paper under "Suspect #2," well aware of the sharp look the sheriff shot his way.

"Motive: He was angry—maybe too angry—that Grace wanted to break up Grace & Favors."

"Ah, shit," Weaver said softly, under his breath, before scrubbing a hand over his face. He knew full well that it was motive enough. The perceived wrong done to a loved one. Especially where money was concerned.

And while Clay had looked genuinely distraught when he'd arrived at the barn, it could just as easily have been from guilt at having killed Grace and worry about getting caught, as from finding out that she'd *been* killed if he were innocent.

Couple that with the fact he'd been the first responder, which Wes always found suspect when the cop in question had been involved with the victim, and his steadfast refusal to take so much as a peek at the crime scene before rushing up to the house to get away from it, put him firmly on the suspect list as far as Wes was concerned. Even though both of those things could also go either way, guilty or innocent.

"Suspect #3, Peter Sutcliff."

Harry looked up in surprise, her mouth making a little "O" as she realized what it meant, before she added his name to the last sheet.

"Don't think I know him," the sheriff said, frowning.

"He works for another local dyer, Daphne Goshart," Harry told him.

"And he's got a motive?"

Wes nodded. "Apparently he had thing for Grace."

"And let me guess, she wasn't interested," the sheriff said, sighing. He stared morosely at the three suspect sheets before shaking his head. "Jealousy is as good a motive as the rest of them."

The fact Peter had never asked exactly what had happened at Grace's, was also interesting in and of itself to Wes. Especially since Peter hadn't seemed in the least bit upset that something *had* happened. Either he was a stone-cold killer, or he genuinely hadn't known that Grace was dead yet and had thought whatever had happened had been inconsequential.

"All right, what do you have next?"

"Alibis," Wes and Harry said together.

The sheriff snorted. "Got this down pat, haven't you?"

"It took a while," Harry told him with a smile, no doubt

remembering how she and Wes had butted heads the first time they'd looked at the "facts" of a murder together.

"Alibis it is, then."

"Or lack of them," Wes said, which drew a sharp look from the sheriff.

CHAPTER TWENTY-TWO

"Meredith," Wes said, starting back at the beginning again. "We know she was in her kitchen somewhere between eight o'five or so and eight-twenty, because she was on the phone talking to Grace and both Janine and Ellen verified it.

"Then, according to Meredith, when she was done talking to Grace, she went out to her compost bin and then came back inside and took a shower. Ellen confirmed she saw her in the backyard around eight-twentyfive. But we only have her word for it, since Janine was either taking a shower herself, or was in her room getting dressed .

"The next time we *can* verify Meredith was anywhere, was right around nine, when she held the back door open for Janine, who was leaving to bring the donuts down here to Grace's.

"Which," he went on, "gave her a window of almost thirty-five minutes where no one can account for her whereabouts."

The sheriff shook his head. "Well, that's not good."

Not for Meredith, it wasn't.

"Dale Clay," Wes said next, and from the corner of his eye, he saw Weaver lean forward slightly. "We know he was on the road in front of Grace's house around seven or seven-fifteen this morning, because Ellen Montrose saw him and flagged him down to help her move some things for Goodwill out onto her front porch."

"Did he now?" the sheriff said sourly. "Something else he neglected to tell us. But, from the timing, I'm thinking he was just starting out on his morning patrol."

Wes thought about that for a minute before saying, "Your deputies, they're all having to patrol larger areas right now than they normally would, since you're shorthanded. Am I right?"

"Yes, they're roughly covering twice the territory they should be. So instead of cycling through every hour or so, it's taking them two. Ah, damn it!" Weaver snarled. "Clay should have been at the far end of his patrol when you called in the murder."

"Then how was he the first responder?" Harry asked, frowning up at him.

"Damned if I know, but it's a question I'm surely going to be asking him as soon as we're done here." Weaver growled.

"That's not the question that needs asking," Wes told him. "The right question is, why was his car *in her driveway* at eight-thirty this morning?"

"What the hell?" Weaver exclaimed half getting out of his chair. "Who told you that?"

With a half-feral smile, Wes answered, "Our third suspect."

"Peter Sutcliff?" Harry said, eyes wide in astonishment. "He *told* you he was here?"

"He did. According to him, he drove over to see Grace, but when he got here Dale Clay's car was 'up at the house,' his words, so he drove around for a bit, but when he came back, Clay's car was at the end of driveway, so he just went back to Daphne's."

"And you believe him?" Weaver growled, settling back into his chair again.

"According to the two interns who work for Daphne, he was back at her studio a little before nine, complaining about having to park his car out on the road, so, he'd definitely driven somewhere."

Then, looking over at Harry, he added, "You know what else they told me? He drives a gray Dodge Charger."

"Wait—so the gray Dodge Charger Ellen told us she saw could have been either Clay's or Peter's!" Harry exclaimed.

"Yup," he agreed, with just a hint of a grin.

Harry narrowed her eyes. "You could have told me!"

"I just did," he pointed out, laughing when Harry smacked his arm and said, "Oh, you!"

"So, what you're telling me is, none of them have airtight alibis," Weaver said, sighing as he rubbed his eyes.

"No," Wes said, shaking his head. "What I'm telling you is that none of them *have* alibis and that all three of them had motive and plenty of time to kill Grace too."

"You don't need to look so pleased about it," Harry half whispered, smacking his arm again.

"It's like one of those damn Agatha Christie movies. The ones where everyone's in the same room, then the lights go out, and someone gets killed but no one knows who did it." The sheriff glared at Harry's neatly written sheets. "What we need, is some evidence."

"How about bloody clothes?" Wes asked, grinning broadly.

"Bloody clothes?" the sheriff repeated, giving Wes a hard look.

Wes leaned forward. "This is where things get a little weird."

"Is he always like this?" Weaver asked Harry.

"No. I think he's channeling his partner, Fountain Rhodes. Because Fountain *is* always like this. Define weird now, Wes!" She glared at him.

"According to Sutcliff, when he got back home, he had to change his clothes because he'd 'splashed red dye on them' earlier."

"He happen to say what he did with those clothes?" Weaver asked, eyes fixed on Wes intently, with a grin of his own slipping over his lips.

"Not in so many words. But I think you'll find them on the floor in his apartment. It's not like he had time to get rid of them."

That won Wes a wolfish grin from the sheriff. "And I happen to know a judge who will expedite a search warrant."

Excellent, Wes thought.

"But why would he tell you about them if they were covered in blood?" Harry objected. "That would be stupid."

"Because criminals *are* stupid," the sheriff said gruffly, sending off a text message to someone, presumably to get the request for a warrant moving along.

Harry shook her head, staring at the lists she'd written. "I wouldn't be," she said with certainty.

"What would you have done?" Wes asked.

She tipped her head to the side, considering. "Because she was stabbed, there would have been blood on the killer's clothes, correct me if I'm wrong?"

Weaver nodded. "More than likely."

"So, why tell a 'cop' your clothes were covered in dye unless A: they really were, or B: you knew they'd jump to the conclusion it was blood when you said the dye was red, thereby laying a very nice red herring in the best Agatha Christie tradition."

"I prefer cod," Wes said, which earned him yet another smack from Harry.

Weaver said, "Go on."

"Let's suppose, for just a minute, that Peter is very smart and that he also did it. So, what if, when he got home, Peter knew he had to get rid of the clothes he'd been wearing because they really did have blood on them. So, he spilled red dye on some *different* clothes and then left them conveniently on the floor for you to find, thereby removing himself from your list of suspects because there won't be any blood on *those* clothes for you *to* find."

That's my clever girl, Wes thought.

"Where do you think the clothes he was wearing when he killed Grace are then?" Weaver asked curiously.

"Maybe he found someplace to burn them. Or maybe he just put them in the wash."

"Where we wouldn't look because of the 'blood stained' clothes on the floor."

"Exactly," Harry agreed. "And once you'd taken those, he could get rid of the others at his leisure."

Weaver shook his head. "That was truly convoluted."

"I think brilliant was the word you were looking for," she shot back, with a wink, "but it's also possible."

"Do me a favor, would you?" Weaver said, "don't kill anyone in my jurisdiction. Please?"

"Well, you'd never find out if I did," she told him, smirking.

"That's what I'm afraid of."

"But it does raise an interesting question, don't you think?" Harry said thoughtfully. "The killer would have had blood on their clothing, and, since I'm assuming Dale didn't have any on his uniform when you saw him"—Wes shook his head—"and Meredith didn't have any on hers or Janine would have told you, if either one of them did it, where are their bloody clothes?"

"She just had to ask that didn't she?" the sheriff said, sighing.

It was a good question, Wes thought. A *very* good question, because neither Clay nor Meredith would have had more than a few minutes to get cleaned up and changed before someone saw them.

"When Deputy Clay arrived on the scene, his clothes were clean, right?" Harry asked Wes. "Or you would have noticed."

"They were, yes," Wes agreed. "He was wearing a freshly cleaned uniform. Right out of the bag, I'm thinking, because of the creases in the pant legs."

"He wouldn't happen to live nearby, would he?" Harry asked Weaver.

"Damn it," the sheriff swore softly. "Yes, he does. So, in theory he could have killed her, then gone home, showered and changed, and still had time to be back as the first responder."

"He lives that close?" Wes asked in surprise.

Weaver huffed out a breath. "Not more than two minutes. Three if it's raining." Which it hadn't been.

"Looks like we need a second warrant," Harry told him.

"Which leaves us with Meredith," Wes said thoughtfully, as the sheriff tapped out another message on his phone. "She could have slipped down the path between their houses while Janine was showering, killed Grace, and been home in a matter of minutes. Which means—"

"I need a third warrant," Weaver snarled, back on his phone again, his fingers flying as he sent another text message to whomever was on the other end, again.

For a minute, it was silent as the two men watched Harry get up and cross the kitchen to a shelf where several cookbooks and photographs vied for space with an overenthusiastic Christmas cactus.

"Or," Harry added, glancing at Weaver apologetically, one of the photographs in her hand. "She could have just showered and changed here and then slipped back up to her studio with no one the wiser."

"Because they were the same size," Weaver said, staring down at the picture she handed to him. "And who would think of looking for bloody clothes in the victim's house?" He finished wearily. "You're a menace," he added, glowering at Harry, although she knew he didn't mean it. "Warrant number four coming right up."

"You do realize," Weaver said, when he was done typing, "that I'm going to have to lose to the judge at golf for the next few months because of this, don't you?" Then, with a sigh, he added, "Although it being the weekend and all, tracking him down might take a while."

"In that case," Wes said, standing up and stretching, "I think I'll go back over to Ellen's. See if I can't push her for some more information about Grace's relationships with both Clay and Meredith." And ask her about that damn yarn she was knitting with.

"Wanna come with me?" he asked Harry.

"I wouldn't miss it," she told him, grinning.

"Sounds like a plan," Weaver said agreeably. "Oh, do me a favor will you? On your way past the barn tell Clay I want to see him. One way or another, I'm going to wring the truth out of that boy about where he really was at eight-thirty this morning."

CHAPTER TWENTY-THREE

"Oh, hello," Ellen said, answering her door with less enthusiasm than Wes expected.

"Bad time?"

"Noooooo." She plastered a smile on her face and let them in. Then she fluttered around them for a minute, pointing them to her wing-backed chairs and offering them either tea or coffee, both of which they declined, before settling down in her place on the couch and picking up her knitting.

"I'm guessing this isn't a social call," she said, fidgeting with the stitches on her needles, sliding them back and forth. "Has something else happened?"

"Not that I know of," Wes answered, eyes narrowing at how nervous the woman was.

And she was, very, picking up her knitting, then setting it down again, fiddling with her yarn, and not quite meeting his eyes as her gaze flitted around the room.

"Ellen, is there something wrong?" Harry asked.

"Oh. Oh no, dear. It's just—" Her shoulders slumped. "Yes, there is actually."

Taking a ragged breath, she raised her chin, straightened her shoulders, looked Wes in the eye, and said, "I might not have been quite as truthful as I should have been about where I saw Dale this morning, before I flagged him down in the road," she admitted. "But I—I just didn't want to get him into trouble."

"And just where, exactly, did you really see him?" he asked, barely keeping his voice calm and steady, when what he really wanted to do was yell at her instead.

Stupid woman.

"He was parked at the end of Grace's driveway, like he'd been up at the house before and now was just sitting there, thinking about something. It was a minute or two later before he turned out into the road, and I flagged him down to come help me."

Wes thought through what she'd said, not sure how it changed anything, since Grace would have still been alive when he left.

"But it was still around seven a.m. when you saw him?" Wes confirmed.

She nodded. "At the most just a little bit after."

"And how did he seem, when he was helping you?" Harry asked her.

Ellen tilted her head to the side. "Sad, I think, and maybe a little angry. They used to date, you know. In fact, they'd only just broken up. I think she might have caught him cheating, not that she actually ever told me that. It was just an impression I got.

"They'd had this huge fight. I could hear it all the way over here, not the words, but the shouting, because both our windows were open. It was one of those lovely warm days we had a few weeks ago, right after that snow, where the weather went from twenty to seventy practically overnight? Anyway, at the end of the shouting I heard her yell, 'How could you?' and then she threw him out."

"He was living there?" Wes asked, leaning forward.

Ellen shook her head vehemently. "Oh no! I didn't mean to imply that. Although he did stay overnight, if you know what I mean, and more than once or twice.

"Not that I was checking, you understand, but that's something you notice. The deputies take their patrol cars home, and I saw it there late at night and still there early in the morning on several different occasions."

He just bet she did, and beside him, Harry turned a snort into a little cough.

"I'm sorry I lied, Agent Smith. I just didn't want Dale to get in trouble with Sheriff Weaver. I didn't know how he'd take it, seeing as how Dale and Grace weren't *married*."

That proved too much for Harry. She bolted from the room down the hallway into, what Wes presumed was a bathroom, where her snorts of laughter could be mistaken for a violent fit of coughing.

"Oh dear, I really do hope Harriett isn't coming down with

anything," Ellen said worriedly. "She's got such a terrible cough."

Only around you, Wes thought irritably.

Then, putting a little steel into his voice, Wes asked, "So later, *after* you left the barn and came home to change, did you really see a car driving away down the road?"

She nodded emphatically, sure of herself. "Yes. I did. A gray Dodge Charger."

It could have been either Clay's or Peter's, since he only had Peter's word for it that Clay had really been there. Unless Ellen had seen Clay, too, and had chosen not to tell him for some other convoluted reason.

Leaning forward, just a bit, Wes narrowed his eyes and let a tiny glimpse of his inner thug shine through. Time for the truth, Ellen. "Did you see Dale Clay at any other time this morning after he helped you put out your bags for Goodwill?"

Her eyes got almost comically wide for a second, before she covered her mouth with her fingertips. "Didn't I tell you? I'm sure I told you," she said with a little frown he wasn't buying. "I saw Dale at the end of Grace's driveway when I left the barn to go home."

Did you now?

"And when was that, exactly?" he asked, letting a little disbelief color his words.

Her nostrils flared. "Eight-twenty a.m. exactly. Because that's when I left the barn," she told him, throwing his words right back at him.

Biting back a little grin, he leaned back in his chair, letting his thugginess slide away.

Okay then.

And then she threw everything for a loop.

"And I've been thinking about when exactly I saw that car," she continued, "and I think it must have been around eight-forty-five a.m. or so, because it doesn't take me that long to shower, and I saw it just shortly after."

Wes blinked. What?

Then it couldn't have been Peter's car. Because if she really had seen him at eight-forty-five, then he wouldn't have had time to make it back to Daphne's, change his clothes and be in her shop by nine a.m. when Adam and China had seen him.

The drive alone would have eaten up all that time.

So, it had to have been Clay, unless she was lying about *when* she'd seen the car drive by? But why would she? Her other lies had been more along the lines of "sins of omission."

Damn it, the woman was giving him a headache.

"Okay, let me get this straight. So, you saw Dale Clay around eight-twenty in Grace's driveway."

"Yes."

And Peter Sutcliff had seen Clay there around eight-thirty a.m.

"Then you saw a gray Dodge Charger out on the road about eight-forty-five a.m."

"Yes."

So, if it had been Clay, where had he gone in the missing

fifteen minutes? Home to change his bloody clothes if he'd been the one who'd killed Grace?

Something he'd know soon enough, once the warrants came in. Or when Weaver got the truth out of him.

Time to move on.

"You mentioned Grace was upset when you first got to the barn this morning," he said, letting it go and changing direction.

"Do you think it might have been because she'd seen Dale earlier?" he asked, trying to keep his voice pleasant, even though what he wanted to do was strangle her.

Ellen hesitated a minute, like she was thinking about it, brows drawn tightly together. "Yes. Now that you mention it, I do, and of course it only got worse when Meredith called. Which is why I left. I didn't want to hear them yelling at each other again."

Again? Wes thought. Why would she say Meredith called Grace when he knew it was the other way around. Why lie about that too?

"What makes you think it was Meredith who called Grace?" He was curious to hear her answer.

"Because she was upset about the business."

"What about the business?" Wes asked, leaning forward slightly.

"About breaking it up, of course. No," Ellen shook her head, as if annoyed with herself. "No," she repeated more firmly. "It was about breaking the *name* up, which was something I know Grace wanted to do and Meredith didn't."

Something that had been ongoing, which Meredith had also told him.

But what if something had changed today? What if Grace had finally put her foot down about breaking up Grace & Favors, and Meredith had snapped?

Had she come down to the barn to confront her about it? Maybe pleaded with her not to go through with it and when Grace had stood firm, had killed her?

Or, had Dale gone to Grace's house early this morning to plead with her on Meredith's behalf then, being told no, had he stewed about it for a couple of hours and then come back and killed her?

Or maybe the gray Dodge Charger Ellen had seen really had been Peter's driving away after *he'd* killed Grace, and he'd lied about seeing Clay in the driveway at eight-thirty, and Ellen had just gotten the time wrong.

Wes blew out an irritated breath.

What he needed to know was where Clay had really been that morning. He had a feeling that knowing that would answer a lot of questions. But a surreptitious glance at his phone confirmed that Weaver hadn't messaged him yet.

"Oh! Harriett, there you are, dear. I was starting to get worried," Ellen exclaimed, as Harry came back into the living room. "Are you feeling better now?"

Somehow managing to keep a straight face, she nodded and said, "It was just a little tickle, and I didn't want to be coughing over Wes, while he was trying to talk to you."

"How very thoughtful of you, my dear," Ellen told her.

While Wes thought, dear god, she had to be acting. This could not be for real.

Then, just a little hesitantly, Ellen asked, "Agent Smith, I was wondering, do you—do you have any suspects yet? I mean, it's just that I'm all alone out here, especially now that Grace is gone, without so much as even a cat." Her hands stilled on her knitting. "Should I go stay with a friend, perhaps? Until you catch the killer, that is?"

Harry cleared her throat several times, trying unsuccessfully not to laugh, finally giving in to a violent bought of coughing into the tissue she had gripped in her hand.

"Sorry, sorry, I'm all right," she said, wiping at her eyes.

Wes nodded, "Yes, that might be a good idea," he agreed resolutely keeping his eyes on Ellen. "Just let one of the officers next door know where you'll be, in case we have any more questions for you."

"Oh yes, of course," Ellen nodded. "I'll just call my friend and pack up a few things." Suiting actions to words, she started to stuff her knitting into the large cloth bag at her feet.

Knitting that suddenly caught Wes's attention.

"That's unusual yarn isn't it?" he asked, staring hard at it. It was the same yarn she'd been knitting with the last time he'd been there. He just hadn't paid much attention to it then.

But it had his attention now, because even all wound up into a cake like that, he could see tiny red speckles and what looked like larger red splotches scattered across it. But was it the same yarn that he'd seen hanging in Grace's barn?

Yarn, that according to Janine, couldn't happen. *Unless someone had thrown red dye over it?*

Ellen stroked it lovingly, before tucking it away out of sight.

"Yes," she agreed, "very unusual. We were going to sell it at the dye crawl. We dyed it especially, you know."

Wes frowned. So maybe Janine had been wrong? Maybe it was something she just hadn't learned how to do yet because it was something Grace did but Meredith didn't?

"I took a couple of skeins to play with, this morning, because it was just so pretty."

So, it *was* the same yarn, then, only without the blood spatter and dye thrown on it.

"Only now what I'm making will be a memorial to Grace, since it will be the last yarn she'll ever have created."

Which was, Wes thought, a very odd way of putting it.

CHAPTER TWENTY-FOUR

"Didn't you drive?" Ellen asked, looking around for their car as she followed Wes and Harry out onto her front porch.

Wes shook his head. "No, it just seemed easier to walk, what with you being right next door."

"And you probably came the long way, up and down the driveways." She tisked. "It'll be faster going back if you take the secret path," she said, with a wink at Wes. "No point in going the long way around again if you don't have to. Come on." Opening the screen door again, she ushered them back into her house.

Dutifully, they followed her back through the living room, down the hallway, then across her tiny kitchen, coming out on her back stoop where the unmistakable smell of something burning met Wes's nose.

Pulling back from the hug she just given Ellen, Harry made a gagging noise. "Ugh, those are the nastiest smelling leaves I've ever smelled," she exclaimed. "What are they?"

Ellen turned to look across the yard, a puzzled expression on her face as she sniffed the air. "I have no idea. I wonder who—" And then her voice trailed off as her eyes settled on the burn barrel at the back of her yard, where a steady trickle of smoke danced and swayed above it.

"But I'm not burning anything!" she exclaimed, stepping off the backdoor stoop and setting off toward it.

Wes and Harry exchanged a quick look before hurrying after her.

Waving the smoke out of the way, Ellen peered into the burn barrel before taking a step back and coughing. "I have no idea *what's* in there!" Then coughing again, she added, "I can't see past the smoke."

Whatever was in there was burning slowly, Wes thought, stepping up beside her. Which suggested to Wes that it was wet, or had gotten wet, if there had been any water in the bottom of the barrel when it had been tossed in. And seeing as how it had been raining just a few days before, that seemed more than likely. As to *what* was burning—Wes held his breath as he waved the smoke away and peered through it.

"Can you see what it is?" Harry asked anxiously, keeping well away and upwind, Wes noticed, smiling to himself.

"No, not really."

What he *could* see were a pile of leaves and something white, crumpled at the bottom of the barrel, all smoldering where they weren't soaked through with dirty rainwater or wet ash.

Stepping back, he looked around for something to fish the

white thing out with. Spotting a long, forked stick laying nearby on the ground, he picked it up. Then, leaning over the barrel, he prodded the smoldering contents before lifting out a partially charred white shirt with splashes of red across it.

"Wes," Harry half whispered, shocked. "That must be the shirt the killer was wearing!"

"Then, that's—that's Grace's blood on it!" Ellen added, hand over her mouth, horrified at the thought of it.

"Looks that way," Wes agreed. "And Peter Sutcliff was wearing a white shirt this morning, according to the interns," he added, lips curving in satisfaction.

"A white shirt he claims he splashed red dye on and tossed on the floor of his apartment when he got home. Any bets as to whether they'll find one there when they serve the warrant?"

"But that's not Peter's shirt," Ellen exclaimed. "It's mine!" she told him, a shocked expression racing across her face. "It was in the bag of clothing for Goodwill we set out on my front porch this morning."

Wes blinked. What the hell?

"You're sure?"

"I—yes. There was a small blue stain on the inside of the back collar, and I can see it from here. But I don't—I don't understand what it's doing here. I don't understand how it *got* here!"

Moving up beside her, Harry took the shocked woman's hand.

"Ellen, who else besides you and Deputy Clay knew there were donations waiting for Goodwill on your front porch?" she asked.

Ellen frowned. "Well, no one." Then her eyes flew open wide as she realized what she'd just said. "Dear god, you don't think *he* took it, do you? That he—that he put it on over his uniform, then killed Grace and tossed it in my burn bin to get rid of the evidence when he realized there was blood on it?" she asked, horrified.

Wes took a moment to think it through, but something about it just didn't quite add up. Why discard evidence in a place you knew it might be found and would point directly *at* you if that happened?

"No, I don't" he told her, and for just a second, he thought he saw a flash of annoyance in her eyes.

"Then I just don't know. Who would do such a thing? Who would take it? Who would have—" And then she paused, her eyes going impossibly wide. "Oh no, if the killer took it, that means they were on my porch! Oh my god," she half whispered, wrapping her arms around herself and shivering at the thought of it.

Not a heartwarming idea, Wes agreed.

Then, as gently as he could, he said, "Ellen, I'm sorry, but as of right now your back yard and front porch are officially crime scenes. I need you to go back inside your house and stay there until I can send a CSI to take your prints and get a DNA swab.

Just so we can clear you, in case the killer left any evidence," he added as her eyes widened slightly.

"Oh my," she half whispered, a hand going to her throat as two little pink spots appeared, one on either cheek.

Wes couldn't decide if it was because she was anxious or excited at the prospect.

"Yes, I can do that," she told him faintly.

"Good. And once that happens, you're free to go to your friend's house."

"As long as I tell an officer where I'm going, first," she said, nodding, but her eyes were fixed firmly on the burn barrel and the shirt that had come from it. And somehow Wes didn't think she was going anyplace, not when she was smack dab in the middle of a murder investigation with a front-row seat.

Watching her walk away, Wes reached for his phone and speed dialed the sheriff.

"What do you have for me Wes?" Weaver asked, coming straight to the point.

"A bloody shirt," he answered.

For a moment, the line was silent before the sheriff bit out, "Another one? Where?"

"Right next door." As quickly as possible, Wes brought the sheriff up to date on what they'd found.

"I'll get a couple of CSIs headed over there right now, and

I've got a couple of deputies I can shake loose from the barn to take over from you, too, so you're not wasting your time standing guard over there."

"Appreciate it." Wes said, before he added, "and did you—" but that was as far as he got before the sheriff cut him off.

"Gotta go. Grace's folks are pulling up the driveway. I'll check back in with you later. See how you're doing." And the line went dead before Wes could ask him if he'd managed to get an answer out of Clay as to where he'd really been at eight-thirty that morning.

Well, damn it, Wes thought, running a hand through his hair. His fingers had just started to tug on the strands when he noticed Harry watching him, a smile creeping across her lips. With a jerk he pulled his fingers back and jammed his hand into a pocket instead.

Damn woman, he thought, not meaning it.

And with a wink, she blew him a kiss.

"Come here, you," he mock growled at her.

"Wes, that is so not appropriate!"

"No, it never is," he agreed, grinning as he pulled her close and very softly, pressed his lips against hers.

"So, who did it, Red?" he asked, resting his forehead against hers.

"Damned if I know," she told him, wrapping her arms around him. "Maybe it's time we looked at everything we know again, see if anything new jumps out at us."

Why the hell not? Wes thought. Then movement down at the barn caught his eye, as a pair of deputies came out through the barn door, said something to Jeb, and started walking toward them. With a regretful little sigh, he gave Harry another kiss, then stepped away from her, all business again.

CHAPTER TWENTY-FIVE

"So, did you find another body?" a cheerful voice asked from directly behind Wes, scaring him half to death.

Turning slowly, he gave Janine a long hard look before saying, "No, we didn't, and how did you know anything was going on over here, anyway?"

She rolled her eyes. "Really?"

"Yes, really," Wes agreed, eyeing her suspiciously. He didn't like the little smirk that dimpled her cheeks. Really didn't like it, when the smirk turned into a full-blown grin.

"First clue," she said, holding up her index finger, "people in hazmat suits." She nodded toward the crime-scene tech, who was poking around in the burn barrel.

"Second clue, yellow crime-scene tape." A second finger joined the first as she gestured at the yellow tape fluttering in the wind.

"Third clue, a conspiracy of cops," she said, indicating the deputies who had joined Harry and Wes in the backyard. "Or wait, that isn't right," she said, frowning. "That's a conspiracy of ravens." Then, tapping a finger against her chin, eyes dancing across his face, she asked, "What *do* you call a gathering of cops? Oh, yeah," she said, her grin widening even more until it covered her whole face. "A donut shop!"

"Janine, be nice," Wes said sternly, even as he fought back a grin of his own. Harry burst out laughing, because it had been pretty clever.

But then, she was a clever kid.

"Sorry, Muscles," she snickered, plainly not sorry at all.

Pinching the bridge of his nose, he shook his head. "No more games," he told her, his voice a little sharper now. "How did you know we were here?"

Huffing out a breath, the teen rolled her eyes again, then pointed up the hill behind them. "I could see you from the kitchen so I came to see what was happening."

Frowning, Wes looked in the direction she'd pointed. Sunlight winked off a pane of glass across the fields. He hadn't realized Meredith's place had a clear view of Ellen's. As well as Grace's. And vice versa, he realized thoughtfully, looking back at Ellen's house again, where he thought he caught movement in her kitchen window. Not too surprised that she was glued to it, watching them.

Which led him to his next question.

"How well do you know Grace's partner?" he asked the blue-haired teen, catching at the edges of something that wasn't quite right. Something that kept slithering away from him.

She gave him an odd look, then shook her head, as if to say, "Grownups," before shrugging. "Pretty well, I guess? I mean she's been a friend of Uncle Aiden's forever, but I've only gotten to really know her well these last few days, since I've been here."

Wes blinked. Wait. *Aiden* knew Ellen? How would he know her—which is when he realized they'd gotten their wires crossed. "I didn't mean Meredith. I meant Ellen."

Janine burst out laughing. "What made you think Ellen was Grace's partner? She was more like her stalker."

"Because she said she was?" Harry told her, exchanging a puzzled look with Wes.

Wes nodded. "She specifically used the word 'partner' when she was talking about her relationship with Grace," he agreed.

"Only in her dreams," Janine snorted.

Wes looked back toward the kitchen window, but there was no one there now.

"Are you sure, Jan?" he asked Janine carefully. "I know that Grace and Meredith weren't partners legally, that they only shared a business name, but Ellen made it sound very much as if she and Grace were working together now."

"Yeah. I'm sure. Trust me, she was stalking Grace, not working with her. Working 'for' her, maybe, but definitely not 'with' her."

"Stalking?" Harry asked, beating Wes to it.

"Yeah, super creepy stalking," Janine said nodding.

Why would anyone stalk a dyer? Wes huffed out a breath. He could understand if his partner, Fountain, had a stalker for instance, since he was dating a movie star and people got angry about things like that. Or if his girlfriend, Molly, had one because she *was* a movie star, and it happened.

But a dyer? Really? A yarn dyer?

He shook his head. Why couldn't knitters behave like normal people? It wasn't that normal people didn't have stalkers, because they did. Jealous ex-boyfriends, or wanna-be boyfriends or angry ex-employees—the list went on and on.

But Ellen was none of those things.

Sure, she was a fan by her own admission. But how did being a yarn dyer's fan lead to murder, unless she, what? Refused to sell you yarn? Which seemed unlikely.

And in Ellen's case, that seemed especially unlikely, since she'd been working with Grace, and you didn't normally invite your stalker to work with you, or for you, or whatever it was that Ellen had done for Grace.

So, maybe Janine was wrong? Or maybe there was something Janine knew she hadn't told them, yet.

"What makes you think Ellen was stalking Grace?" he asked curiously.

"You mean besides the fact I saw it firsthand? How about the fact Grace told Meredith it was getting out of hand?"

"It?"

Janine nodded. "The whole 'helping out' thing."

"How is 'helping out' stalking?"

"Like this, and pay attention," Janine added wiggling her fingers in front of him, as Wes's eyes drifted over to an investigator carrying several bagged items as he came toward them from the front of Ellen's house.

The Goodwill bags, he thought, idly, while saying, "I am."

Janine rolled her eyes and shot Harry a grin. "How about we go back to Meredith's and get something hot to drink, and I'll tell you all about it?"

"Works for me," Harry agreed, and as the two of them turned to go, Janine called out, "Coming, Muscles?"

"What?" He looked around at them before his gaze drifted back to the CSI again. "I'll catch up in a minute." Then, "Wait! where are you going?"

"To Meredith's," Janine told him.

"Okay, good. I'll meet you there in a minute. I just need to talk to the crime-scene tech first."

And as he hurried away, he thought he heard her say, "Of course you will," and then both Janine and Harry laughing.

CHAPTER TWENTY-SIX

"I believe you were going to tell us how you stalk a dyer," Wes said a short time later, coffee cup in hand as he, Harry, and Janine settled around Meredith's kitchen table. The orange cats twined between their legs, looking for food and complaining when none was forthcoming.

"Go, scat!" Janine told them. "You've had your breakfast, and it's not time for your dinner yet." And, as if they understood her, they stalked off, tails held high, back to the living room, grumbling loudly to each other.

Out in the parking area, cars were crammed into every conceivable spot. Meredith was in her shop, taking care of her new customers.

"It starts out innocently enough," Janine began, looking from Wes to Harry and then back again. "You're at a yarn show and you get to talking to a vendor whose yarn you like. Maybe you buy some. Or, maybe you haven't bought any yet, because you're still trying to make up your mind, so you go back several more times and just pet the yarn."

Harry grinned. "Guilty as charged," she said with a laugh.

"Yeah, it happens all the time, especially if it's a two- or three-day show." Janine agreed. "Eventually, you buy some. Then maybe you go back and buy more the next day, because you really, really like it," she continued.

This time, it was Wes who grinned. If he remembered rightly, Harry had bought yarn three times from the same vendor at the show he'd gone to with her.

"And the dyer calls you by name when she thanks you, because it's on your credit card, and it makes you happy."

"Ouch. And here I thought I'd made an impression!" Harry said.

"How many times did you go back to the same booth and actually *buy* something, not just pet the yarn?" Janine asked.

"Maybe threeeeeeee times," she answered, drawing it out.

"Then *you*, the vendor would remember."

"At the next show you go to, you go back to her booth, and the vendor says something like, 'hi, good to see you again,' because she vaguely remembers you. Or, maybe she says, 'Hi, Harry!' because you bought so much yarn from her at the last show, how could she *not* remember you?"

"People are going to be calling out, 'Hi Harry,' all over the next show we go to then," Wes said, which earned him a smack on the arm from Harry.

"No, they're not!"

"Yes, they are," both Wes and Janine told her.

"You do know that it's not going to get any better at the next show, right? That Harry's going to buy the place out again," Janine told him earnestly, trying to hide a grin.

Wes nodded. "Yeah. I'm thinking of getting a trailer, so we have room to bring back her haul," he answered. A grin of his own danced across his lips.

"Okay, maybe I got a *little* excited at my first fiber festival," Harry admitted.

Wes leaned in to give her a little kiss. "Nothing wrong with that, babe."

He turned to Janine. "So what happens next in your 'how to make a stalker' movie?"

Janine shook her head. "He's not taking me seriously, is he?"

"Keep going. Let's see where this ends."

"Fine. Okay. So, the vendor has just called you by name, and you can't help but be a little thrilled, right?"

Harry nodded.

"But that doesn't make you best buds. Unless you're Ellen," she added under her breath, again.

"Then you buy more yarn from her at the show after that, because yarn shows are addictive, and you go to every one you can get to, whether you need more yarn or not."

Wes slid a sidelong glance at Harry and grinned when she stuck her tongue out at him. Yeah, he could see Harry doing that.

With him along to carry whatever she'd bought.

His heart thumped.

"And maybe at *this* show you chat a little more and find out you live in the same city," Janine went on, "which you laugh about because this particular show? It's clear across the state."

"Then summer happens, and there aren't any shows for a while, and by the time they're starting up again, you're anxious to go to one."

"Wait, there aren't any shows in the summer?" Wes asked, surprised.

"No, thank god. Not around here, anyway. We have to rest sometime! I mean, it's pretty nonstop from September through March, with some time off between Christmas and the beginning of the year. Besides not many people want to look at wool when it's like a hundred and twelve degrees outside."

She had a point.

"Anyway, something different happens at this next show.

"At *this* show the dyer sees you and flags you down, because she's desperate to go to the bathroom but doesn't want to leave her booth unattended, and you're a familiar face. So she asks you if you could just hang out for a moment, and you're happy to do it.

"It happens all the time, at every show. Not many vendors travel with a helper or can grab someone like me who's at the show with a family member, knows the business, and is free to booth sit if you ask her nicely."

"Or bribe her with hot fudge sundaes," Wes said, knowing

she loved them. It was something he'd discovered the first time he'd met her.

"Or bribe her with hot fudge sundaes," Janine agreed, smirking. "So they only have three choices, really, when they can't wait any longer to pee.

"They can ask the vendor in the booth next door to keep an eye on things and hope they don't get suddenly busy. They can leave the booth empty and risk someone stealing something—which happens all the time. Or, they can grab a buyer they sell to regularly.

"But that doesn't make you BFF's forever, and most customers understand that. Unless you're Ellen."

"Still not seeing anything stalkerish, yet," Wes told her.

"That's because I'm just getting to the weird bit. Quit interrupting!"

"Yes, ma'am."

Janine rolled her eyes.

"Do I look like a "ma'am" to you?" she asked Harry. "Maybe you need to get his eyes checked. Anyway, then Ellen started showing up at more and more shows.

"Two or three in a season, okay. Nothing weird about that. But every one of them? Ugh, no! Especially when some of them were out of state, hours away.

"And it wasn't like she was even shopping. She was mostly just hanging around Grace, getting her cold drinks when she was thirsty or manning her booth for her during potty breaks. Not that Grace minded the help or anything, it was just weird that Ellen was at every, single, show, like she worked for Grace, or something.

"Then, I had a front row seat for what happened next."

She paused for breath and a slurp of coffee before plowing on.

"We were at this show, and it was the end of the day. Uncle Aiden was done teaching and we were hanging out with a friend of ours in her booth right across from Grace's. Melody, Melody Campbell? You've met her right?"

Wes nodded. They had, at the fiber fair where they'd met Janine.

"It was getting on late in the day, you know, when you start thinking about where to go for dinner? And, Melody suggested we go to this Thai place – which is sooooo good, love their red curry, then she goes over to invite Grace to join us, because we knew she was alone at the show."

"And let me guess, Ellen was there," Harry said, listening raptly.

"Yup," Janine said, popping the "p" loudly.

"So Melody asks Grace to join us, and Ellen butts in before Grace can reply and says *we'd* love to. And then there was this weird kind of pause with Ellen just beaming and Melody looking at Grace like – what? But it was kind of a done deal."

"Talk about awkward," Harry said.

"Seriously. I mean, she just invited herself along but what could Grace do about it? Then, when Ellen showed up at the restaurant she finagled a seat right next to Grace."

"Okay, that's starting to get creepy," Harry said squirming a little.

"Right? And she was all like, 'Oh I'm helping out Grace,' when the person on her left asked her who she was. I don't think Grace realized, since she was talking to the person on her *other* side. And me, I'm sitting opposite them and about all I could do was roll my eyes."

"Not something most people would do," Wes agreed. "Delusional, even, maybe. But still not stalking."

"Maaaaybe. But then it got worse."

Harry shifted uncomfortably, "How could it get worse?"

Janine grinned. "Ellen kept showing up at all these other shows and staying to the bitter end to help Grace pack up."

"But, why would Grace let her?" Harry asked.

"Because, by the end of a show, you're tired and worn out, and you just want to get home. So, honestly? Any and all help is gratefully appreciated. Even from a seriously weird fan," Janine told her.

"Then Grace made a really huge mistake. She wished out loud that Ellen could help her set up too."

"Why would she *do* that?" Harry asked, horrified.

"Because she meant it," Janine said, sighing. "Setting up is even worse than taking down. You have to deal with getting all your stuff into wherever you're showing, first.

"And then you have to deal with booths that aren't the right size, or, walls that wobble or missing lights. It can be pretty awful.

"Having someone there to help is like a blessing in disguise. Even if it is your weird stalker fan."

"And let me guess, Ellen said she could," Wes said dryly.

"Yeah, and then one thing led to another. Ellen started going to shows with Grace. Well, not actually traveling with her. But going on her own, so she could be there to help her setup and teardown. And to help out when her booth got crowded.

"You know, like wrapping up yarn, writing receipts, answering questions, just being an extra set of hands. And it's such a relief to have someone do that because you're back in the corner running credit cards and you can't.

Okay, Wes had to agree, that was really kind of – odd, but still not in the realm of stalking, especially since Grace wasn't objecting.

"And then," Janine said with a flourish, eyes fixed on Wes, "the house went up for sale right next door to Grace, and Ellen pounced on it. And before she'd even unpacked, she was over at the dye studio, 'helping out.'

"Is that 'stalker' enough yet for you?" she added with a smirk.

It was getting close. Especially since, while the story was the same one Ellen had told them, Janine's recounting was far more disturbing.

"It's seriously weird," he allowed.

"Enough to make her a suspect?" the teen pushed.

Was it?

Wes flashed on the burn barrel with Ellen's shirt smoldering in it. A shirt she claimed to have last seen on her front porch in a

Goodwill bag. And on the little flash of anxiety she'd shown when he'd mentioned the DNA swab.

But, what possible reason could she have had to kill Grace? She was living the dream, hanging out with Grace every chance she got. Unless something catastrophic had happened in those last few moments when they'd been together in the barn, he couldn't think of a single thing.

Still . . ..

"Enough to make her a person of interest," he told her.

"Oh, pfft," Harry said with a little shiver, side-eyeing him. "She bought the freaking house *next door,* Wes! That totally makes her a suspect."

Reaching into her purse, she pulled out all their previous notes and then her pad and pencil, tore off a fresh sheet, and at the top of it wrote:

"Suspect #4"

And right beneath that, "Ellen Montrose" in big bold letters.

CHAPTER TWENTY-SEVEN

Okaaaaay, Wes thought, leaning back in his chair, so he'd been overruled by a feisty red head and a teen with blue hair. Fair enough. She had a point. As much as he wanted to deny it, Janine was right. Ellen had crossed the invisible line from fan to stalker when she'd bought the house next door.

And stalkers had a very bad habit of killing the person they were stalking. The only question now was: what possible reason could Ellen have had to kill Grace?

Running his hand through his hair, he gave the top a little tug, watching as Harry methodically laid out the suspect sheets they already had and just as methodically Janine picked each one up and read it.

In the real world, Wes would have stopped her, since she wasn't law enforcement, or a consultant, which is how he thought of Harry. But he didn't, because she wasn't your average teen, and, as she'd just proven, sometimes she saw things the "grownups" didn't. In fact, she had helped him catch a killer the first time they'd met.

"Who's this?" she asked, suddenly, tapping a finger on Peter's page as she squinted up at him.

"Daphne Goshart's PA, who was interested in Grace, only she wasn't interested in him," he told her.

"Unrequited love," she said, nodding, before going back to staring at the papers laid out in front of her.

That was one way to put it, Wes thought, biting back a grin. He had a feeling this semester's English class had Shakespeare's name written all over it.

Putting down the last sheet she'd been reading, she rubbed her jaw thoughtfully and said, "So, what we have here are, a stalker, if you include Ellen—"

"We're definitely including Ellen," Harry said firmly.

"Okay," Janine agreed. "So we have a stalker, a spurned lover, an ex-boyfriend and a whatever Merry is. Except, Merry didn't do it," she added loyally. "Although," she admitted, slumping back in her seat, "if you were just looking at the facts as you have them here, she could have."

Wes blinked. Playing back what the teen had just said.

The facts as they had them . . .

But what if the facts were wrong?

Something tugged at Wes's mind. Something about the time-line. He frowned trying to catch hold of it, but it slithered back to wherever it had been when Harry's cheerful voice said, "All right! Time to fill in the blanks on Ellen's suspect sheet and see what we see."

She picked up her pencil and wrote "Motive" under the woman's name.

For a minute, they just stared at each other blankly, before Harry said, "We'll come back to that one, later, shall we?"

"Next, alibi."

She wrote it on the line under "Motive."

"She doesn't actually have one of those either, does she?" Harry said, looking up at Wes in surprise.

"We need to check that she wasn't shopping online or on the phone around the time Grace died, then," Janine said, helpfully.

"That would only happen if this were a TV show," Wes said darkly. And then he caught her smirk. No. Not her too. He shot her a disgusted look and delighted, Janine blew him a kiss.

"So sue me, I *like* those shows. All those hunky guys running around in dark suits and shades," she teased.

"Focus," he ordered. She snorted out a laugh.

"Oh, trust me, I do. Especially when they take off their shirts."

"Give me strength," he muttered.

"Opportunity," Harry said, ignoring them both as she added the word below "Alibi."

"Crap," Janine swore. "This isn't working."

Wes blinked, and then smiled. "You, Jan, are brilliant," he told her.

"Well, yeah? But um—care to explain to the rest of the class?" she added, pointing between herself and Harry.

"We're going about this all wrong. We need to come at it from a different direction."

"Which is?" she prodded.

"We need to look at the timeline again."

"Okaaaay," Janine said doubtfully, while Harry's sharp gaze rested on his face for a moment before she tore a fresh sheet of paper off her pad, laid it in front of her and wrote: "Timeline."

"Ready."

"Okay, let's keep this to bullet points," Wes told her.

"Got it." And checking their "suspect sheets" from time to time she wrote:

7:00 a.m. Clay at Grace's according to Ellen

7:00/7:10 a.m. Clay at Ellen's according to both of them

8:10 a.m. Grace on phone with Meredith according to Meredith and Janine

8:10 a.m. Ellen heard in background of phone call according to Meredith & Janine

8:15 a.m. Clay parked up at Grace's barn according to Peter

8:20 a.m. Grace on phone with Meredith according to Ellen

8:20 a.m. Ellen tells Grace she's leaving to go home according to Ellen

8:20 a.m. Clay at end of Grace's driveway according to Ellen

8:25 a.m. Meredith outside her backdoor according to Ellen

8:30 a.m. Clay at the end of Grace's driveway according to Peter

8:30 a.m. Ellen in the shower according to Ellen

8:30–8:45 a.m. Grace is most likely murdered

8:45 a.m. Ellen sees gray Dodge Charger according to Ellen

9:00 a.m. Janine sees Meredith outside Meredith's backdoor according to Janine

9:00 a.m. Wes & Harry find Grace

9:05 a.m. Clay arrives at Grace's

9 something a.m. Ellen returns to Grace's

Running his eyes over the list, Wes locked in on the entries for Clay.

"Damn it, I need to know why he was at Grace's at both seven a.m. and again a little after eight a.m. this morning," he muttered, eyeing his cell phone and wondering if he could call Weaver back yet.

"Who, Clay?" Janine asked, a little smirk on her face. "Well, that's easy, he was returning his key to her place. Or trying to, anyway," she added carelessly.

Wes looked at her, eyes narrowed.

"Care to run that by me?" he asked, his voice sharp, irritated.

She huffed out a breath. "It's not rocket science," she complained.

When he growled, she glared back at him and snapped, "Fine. Meredith was annoyed with him that he hadn't returned Grace's key to her yet, so she sent him over to do it before breakfast."

Wes blinked, sidetracked.

"Before breakfast?" he echoed.

Janine slid a sideways glance at Harry before answering, "Yes?"

"He was at Meredith's *before breakfast,*" Wes repeated, his voice dancing along the edge of becoming dangerous.

Unfazed, Janine rolled her eyes. "Yeah? He was there all night."

"And you never thought I might need to know that?" he snapped.

She shrugged. "No. Why? What difference does it make?"

Wes took a deep breath, then let it out slowly again, because the answer was none. Whatsoever.

Shit, he was losing it.

He gave his hair a sharp tug, catching back the fragments of the rest of what she'd told him.

"So he was there at seven a.m., but he didn't leave the key. Why not?"

"Because she didn't answer the door for one thing—"

"He could have left it under the mat.

"*And,* for another," she went on, glaring at him for interrupting, "he had some things inside he still needed to get. But he didn't want to just barge in on her if she was like, still sleeping or in the shower. Something like that."

Fair enough.

"Which is why he went back there again around eight-thirty," Wes said nodding in understanding.

Janine shook her head, tapping the page where Harry had written:

8:15 a.m. Peter sees Clay up at Grace's barn.

"Nah, I think it was more like then, eight-fifteen instead of eight-thirty. because he left not long after Grace called. I don't think he really wanted to see her, you know? And since he knew she was in the barn, it seemed safe enough to go back then."

Sneaking in and out when she wasn't looking, Wes thought.

Then, sliding her finger farther down the page to where it read: *8:30 a.m. Clay at end of Grace's driveway*, Janine said, "So this would have been after he'd gotten his stuff."

Which, now that he knew *why* the man had been there, made those fifteen minutes when he'd been missing make perfect sense. He'd probably just been running his things back home. Not killing Grace and cleaning up after. Or at least, that was another possibility.

"But he was still at Meredith's when Grace called," Wes said, mostly to himself, feeling out the new puzzle pieces. Because something was off.

He glared at the timeline, trying to figure out what was bothering him about it. Because something was.

And then he got it.

Peter had seen Dale Clay sitting at the *end* of Grace's driveway at eight-thirty, when Ellen claimed she was showering. But according to Ellen, Clay had been there at *eight-twenty*, except he couldn't have been.

He grinned wolfishly.

"What?" Janine demanded.

"Harry grab a new sheet of paper," he asked her.

She tore one off quickly and waited for him to go on.

"Okay, if Clay didn't leave Meredith's until *after* Grace called, that means he was still there at either, A: eight-ten or B: eight-twenty, depending on who you believe as to *when* she called."

Janine started to complain, but Harry shushed her as she listened.

"And if he left right after she called, that would have put him at the barn at roughly eight-fifteen or eight-twenty-five this morning—depending on which timeline you're following."

Janine nodded.

"Now, according to Peter," Wes went on, "Clay was parked *up at the barn* when he first drove by at eight-fifteen a.m. which fits in with timeline 'A' perfectly. And he was at *the end* of the driveway when Peter went by a short time later at eight-thirty."

"Which also fits timeline 'A' perfectly," Harry said slowly.

"But," Wes said, the corners of his eyes crinkling as he fought back a grin, "according to Ellen, Clay was at the end of Grace's driveway at eight-twenty a.m."

Timeline A:

Phone call according to Janine & Meredith:

8:10 a.m. Fact: Clay was still at Meredith's

According to Peter:

8:15 a.m. Clay at barn

According to Peter:

8:30 a.m. Clay at end of driveway

Timeline B:

Phone call according to Ellen:

8:20 a.m.

According to Ellen:

8:20 a.m. Clay at end of driveway

According to Ellen:

8:20 a.m. left to go home to shower

"But that's not possible," Harry said, shaking her head as she stared at the new list she'd just written. "Because Clay was still at Meredith's when Grace called her.

"Then he couldn't have been at Grace's like Ellen said he was!" Janine exclaimed, excitedly, thumping the list.

"No," Wes agreed, "but *she* didn't know that," he added with a very satisfied grin.

"So she lied!" Janine breathed softly.

"She did." He nodded. "Now the question is why?"

And picking up Ellen's empty suspect page, Wes laid it back in front of Harry, again and said, "I think it's time we start over and fill in all the blanks."

CHAPTER TWENTY-EIGHT

"Okay, motive," Harry said, pencil poised above the paper.

"That's the reason someone commits a crime, right?" Janine asked. "But what possible reason could Ellen have had to kill Grace? I mean she was hanging out around her all the time, living the stalker dream.

"I mean, it wasn't like Grace was going to suddenly throw her out or—oh crap," Janine whispered, eyes going wide. "That's exactly what she was planning on doing!"

Snapping his eyes up to hers, Wes asked, "Jan, what are you talking about?"

"It's what she said, this morning, when she was talking to Meredith. Grace said something like, 'I've had enough. I can't take it anymore.' You don't, you don't think Ellen heard her, do you?"

Ah shit.

Running his hand through his hair, Wes gave it a little tug

before saying, "Yes, I do. Because those are the exact same words Ellen told us she overheard Grace use. Except she told us they were about Meredith."

And under "Motive," pencil scratching away, Harry wrote: If she couldn't have Grace, then nobody could.

Which, Wes thought, was chilling when you saw it there in black and white.

"My god, she did it. She totally did," Janine said, staring at the words.

"Maybe."

"Maybe?" Janine squeaked.

Wes tapped the other suspect lists. "They all had motives, Jan. What we're trying to do here is whittle it down a little."

"But she lied!" the teen said indignantly.

Letting a little steel slide into his voice, Wes said, "And so did everyone else."

"All right, you two, stop bickering," Harry interjected before Janine could get going again. "Next up is alibi. What do we know about where Ellen was this morning?"

Janine glared at Wes for a moment longer before slouching back in her chair and transferring her glare to the paper Harry was writing on. "Um, nothing?"

"Not true," Wes said, tapping the timeline sheet. "We know she was on her front porch at seven this morning, because Clay was there with her."

"And we know she was in the barn with Grace somewhere between eight-ten and eight-twenty, because you heard her voice in the background telling Grace she was going home." He added.

"And—" Wes blinked.

That was it? That was all they knew?

He ran his eyes back over the sheet of paper, but it was oddly blank when it came to where Ellen had been.

And the something that he hadn't quite been able to remember came knocking at Wes's brain again, demanding to be let in. And very slowly a smile slid across his lips.

"So, what's the common denominator in all of these?" he asked, waving his hand across the three other suspect papers.

"Three," Janine snarked, pointing out the obvious.

"The one thing we've been hanging everything on?" Wes went on, ignoring her.

Staring down at the papers in front of her, Harry's eyes suddenly widened as they flicked across each one of them. Then, very slowly, she looked them over again before saying, "That Peter, Clay, and Meredith were all in the vicinity of the barn around the time when Grace was murdered."

Wes grinned. "And who was the person that so conveniently pointed that out to us?"

"Ellen," Harry breathed out quietly.

"And at the time we had no reason to think she'd lied," Wes agreed, removing Ellen's suspect sheet from the table and waving his hand over the rest of them.

"Because you didn't know she was behind door number four!" Janine exclaimed, catching on.

Harry's eyes narrowed. "She was just the nice next-door-neighbor lady who helped out Grace sometimes."

"So we never looked in her direction," Wes said, "because we *knew* where she was around eight-thirty, when Grace was most likely murdered."

With a disgusted curl of her lip Harry said, "Taking a shower, because that's what she told us."

"She set us up right from the start. Carefully twisting the truth as to everyone else's relationships and telling us their whereabouts every time she saw us." Wes said, huffing out an annoyed breath. "And the timeline she spun made it all believable, because how else could she have known where everyone else was?"

"Giving herself the perfect alibi," Harry finished.

Yup. Now all Wes had to do was prove it.

"Okay, let's go get her!" Janine said, bounding out of her chair.

"No can do, kiddo," Wes told her, pulling her back down again.

"Why the hell not, she *killed* Grace!"

"Did she?" he asked seriously.

The teen's mouth fell open in disbelief. "What in the—you can't—is he serious?" she spluttered turning to Harry.

"Yes, hon, he is. I know it looks iron clad, but we have to look at every motive, alibi, and opportunity, so the wrong person isn't arrested."

"This is ridiculous," she muttered, flopping back down into

her chair again. "Fine. Let's get on with it then, *before* Ellen gets away."

"Which leads us to opportunity," Wes said, tapping Ellen's suspect page.

"Ellen knew Clay was at the end of the driveway, because she saw him there when she was leaving the barn," Harry said, checking off the information as she wrote it down against her other lists. Check.

"She saw Meredith from her kitchen window." Check.

"And she saw Peter from her front porch when she took the other bag for Goodwill out not at eight-forty-five like she told us, but at eight-thirty, when she was supposed to have been in the shower." Check.

"So the whole—Clay in the driveway at eight-twenty and Peter in the road at eight-forty-five thing was simply misdirection so we wouldn't question her about being in the shower when she said she was," Harry said.

"Yeah," Wes agreed. "Because pinpointing time of death is almost impossible, and everyone knows that."

"And since Ellen knew where they all really were at eight-thirty, it gave her ample time to go back into the barn and kill Grace, since she knew no one would interrupt her," Janine pointed out.

"And ample time to take a shower after, then conveniently reappear once Grace's body had been found," Harry added darkly. "But we can't prove any of it!"

"No," Wes agreed, eyes sliding over the timeline again, "but what if someone could confirm something else for us?"

"Like what?" Harry asked.

"Like that Ellen was really on her porch around eight-thirty a.m., instead of at eight-forty-five like she told us." He asked with a smirk.

Not waiting for an answer, he pulled out his phone, looked up a number in his notes, and dialed it. Then, putting the call on speaker, he gave Janine a pointed look and held a finger to his lips.

Outraged, she'd just started to object when Peter Sutcliff's very English voice said, "Hello? Who's this? Can I help you?"

"I certainly hope so," Wes told him. "This is Special Agent Smith, and I have a quick question for you."

"Hang on a sec, I can barely hear you," he told them.

They could barely hear him either.

"Okay, that's better. Now, how can I help you?" he asked a few seconds later. The noise in the background having been abruptly cut off, and Wes thought he'd stepped into the little hallway off the shop to get away from it.

"When you were driving by Grace's this morning, right before you left to go back to Daphne's, did you see anyone besides Deputy Clay?"

"N—no. I don't think so. Not on the road, anyway. But I did see someone at the house next door. Not clearly, mind you, as they were just going back inside."

"And that was, when did you say?" Wes asked. Wanting him to confirm what he'd told Wes earlier.

"Ummmmm." They could hear him blow out a breath. "About eight-thirty, maybe?" he said slowly. "It couldn't have been much past eight-thirty-five, at any rate, or I'd never have made it back here before nine."

"Great. Just one more thing. Do you remember if it was a man or a woman you saw on the porch?"

And Wes was relatively sure that all three of them held their breath waiting for what he would say.

"A woman, I'm pretty sure. I just caught a glimpse of her but, um, she had a woman's shape—if you know what I mean? Up front?"

Janine smacked both hands over her mouth and pinched her nose to keep from laughing out loud, and Wes's own mouth twitched just a bit. Even Peter's own very posh voice squeaked just a little in embarrassment. Avoiding Harry's eyes, Wes thanked the man and hung up.

"Stop it, you two," he told them, as Harry dissolved into giggles the second the call was over.

"You know, up front," Janine said, holding her hands up at chest height in front of herself, before howling helplessly.

As funny as it might have been, Wes had no doubt that Peter *had* seen Ellen, since she was, in fact, well endowed, or however you said things like that these days.

"When you two are done?" he said pointedly, as they continued to snort and giggle just a bit.

"Okay," Harry said, wiping a tear away. "So what was Ellen really doing on her porch, since she wasn't showering?"

Wes's grin was feral.

"I'll give you one guess."

Harry tipped her head to the side, thinking. "She wasn't just putting out a bag of clothes for Goodwill, was she?" Harry said in sudden understanding.

Wes shook his head. "No. I think after she did that, after she put the other bag out, she took a shirt *out* of one of the bags. The shirt she wore when she killed Grace, and I think I know someone who can prove it."

And before either Harry or Janine could pepper him with questions, he'd whipped out his phone and had Dale Clay on speaker.

"Clay, it's Wes Smith, did you see anyone after you left Grace her key this morning, when you were sitting down in her driveway?"

There was a long pregnant pause before Clay confirmed what they'd already known by saying, "No, but there was a car out on the road. It kind of slowed down as it came to her driveway, and I thought it was a knitter coming by early, but then it kept going."

"And that was when?"

"About eight-thirty?"

That confirmed what Peter had told them.

"It wouldn't have happened to have been a gray Dodge Charger, would it?" Wes asked dryly.

"Yeah, it was. But it wasn't a police vehicle."

Definitely Peter's then.

"Did you see anyone else?" Wes prodded.

"Not on the road. No."

"But you did see someone?" He pushed.

"Just Ellen Montrose, the next-door neighbor. She was out on her front porch, fussing with the bags for Goodwill I'd put out for her earlier."

"Could she have been taking something out of a bag do you think?"

"I—suppose?" Then after a short pause he added, "You know, I think she was."

"What makes you think that?"

"I saw her hold something up, and then she went back inside her house."

Grinning, Wes said, "thanks," and hung up..

"Can we go arrest her now, please?" Janine begged. "I mean, you can't really think anyone else did it."

No, he didn't.

"I mean, she heard Grace say she wanted Ellen out of her life, couple that with the fact she was a crazy-stalker fan, and it pushed her over the edge. Right?

"And then she *lied* to you about where she really was when Grace was being murdered, and you found her shirt, covered in Grace's blood, in the woman's own burn bin! Is that enough evidence for you yet, Wes?"

Close enough.

CHAPTER TWENTY-NINE

"What do you mean, I can't go with?" Janine demanded, hands on her hips as she stood toe to toe with him.

If it hadn't been so serious, it would have been hilarious. Her diminutive five-feet-nothing warring with his six-foot-three inches.

But Wes knew better than to dismiss her. Height had nothing on outrage. And she was outraged that he was even considering leaving her behind when he went to arrest Ellen.

"Janine, if I have to tie you to a damn chair, I will. I can't be looking over my shoulder to be sure you're safe if she pulls out a gun." That kind of thing never ended well.

At the word "gun," her tirade stopped dead. Because she hadn't considered the possibility that Ellen might have one.

But the crazies always did.

"I need to know you and Harry are safe, so I can do my job. Okay?"

"Okay," she answered in a much smaller voice, and then before he could move away, she wrapped her arms around him as best she could and gave him a hug.

"You be careful, you big lug, you hear me?" she told him.

"Always."

Turning to Harry, he said, "Babe, get Weaver moving on backups, will you? I'm sending his info to your phone, now."

Then with a little kiss on her cheek, he was gone. Out the door and moving across Meredith's big backyard, eyes fixed on the winking pane of glass in Ellen Montrose's kitchen window. Wes reached the burn barrel at the same time as Dale Clay. The smoking remains of the bloody shirt, bagged, tagged, and gone.

"Is she still inside?" Clay asked, hunkering down at his side. Eyes sweeping across the back of the house. The consummate professional now he was no longer a suspect.

"As far as I know," Wes confirmed. Movement caught the corner of his eye. It was Jeb, hurrying towards them. Looking back at Clay he said, "Take Jeb and cover the front," But before Clay could move, Jeb blew their plan to hell.

"Hey, Agent Smith?" He called out. "Miss Ellen's gone. She drove out 'bout two minutes ago. I saw her go myself."

Damn it all to hell.

In the back of his mind, he could hear Janine telling him to get on with it, or Ellen would be gone.

"She didn't happen to say where she was going, did she?" Wes asked, because stranger things had happened. It could be something as simple as a trip to the grocery store, as a trip to say, Bolivia, where they couldn't get their hands on her.

"To a friend in town, I think," Jeb answered. "She said you knew where that was?"

Yeah, no.

Out loud, he said, "She's running."

Beside him Clay grabbed up his radio, putting out an APB for her car without Wes having to tell him to. "She should be considered armed and dangerous." He added.

Meeting the deputy's eyes, Wes nodded. Anything was possible.

"She really kill Grace Harper?" Jeb asked.

"Looks like it."

"Damn. And she made really good oatmeal raisin cookies, too. Guess we won't be getting any more of those down at the station," he added mournfully, with a shake of his head.

Likely not, Wes thought, with a sideways glance at the young deputy.

Then, looking around at the rest of the deputies who had joined them he said, "I want the house secured. Front and back. No one goes in until the CSIs can process it."

Beside him Clay took over, dividing the men and hurrying off with them. Seconds later Jeb's radio sprang to life.

Listening intently, he turned to Wes, excitement in his eyes. "They got her! Up at the roadblock top of Small's Creek. The one the sheriff put up there to keep the yarn people away. Guess she didn't know it was there. The APB call went out just as Finn was getting ready to move his patrol car out of the way so she could get by."

Then, grinning, he asked, "You want, I can give you a ride up there?" Jeb gestured toward his patrol car in Ellen's driveway.

Yes, Wes wanted, very much

"This is all your fault!" Ellen snarled, when she caught sight of Wes. "These idiots would never have caught me. They'd have stumbled around for *weeks* looking at Meredith and Dale Clay and that boy who was sniffing around Grace, before they gave up. Or charged one of them with her murder.

"And I would have taken over that ungrateful bitch's studio! I would have made it great, since she couldn't be bothered to!" Madness gleamed in her eyes. "She was content playing in her little world. *Happy.*" She spat out. "When with my business know how and her talent, we could have created something bigger, better—*huge!*"

Wes blinked. Taken aback by the sudden change in Ellen's personality. Gone was the sweet "old" next-door-neighbor lady, replaced with this screaming harpy.

"But she wouldn't listen. Oh no. Wouldn't even contemplate it, because 'what about Meredith?' Her precious Meredith," she sneered, "who was screwing her boyfriend behind her back. What, you think I didn't know? Who do you think she came to, when the shit hit the fan?

"All boo, hoo, hoo. Like I cared. I wouldn't have cheated on her like her *best friend*. I never would have. *I* was her real friend. *I'm* the one who fetched and carried. *I'm* the one who charmed her customers and mixed her disgusting dyes and cleaned up after her when she made a mess—where was her precious Meredith then, huh? In bed with her boyfriend. Oh, I know she denied it. I now she said they hadn't—but she lied.

"They all lie! The ungrateful little bitches! And Grace, who I bled for, worked my fingers to the bone for, lied too, in the end!" Spittle flew from her lips as she leaned toward Wes, her body twisted around in the confines of the back seat of the patrol car so she could see him. Her pant leg rode up, revealing a blue butterfly tattooed on her ankle.

The same butterfly tattoo that both Grace and Meredith sported. Which was definitely stalkerish enough for Wes.

The crazed woman was still screaming at him. "I heard what Grace said to Meredith. How *I* was driving her crazy and *she'd* had enough *of me!* How she was going to kick *me* out. *Me!* After everything I'd done for her. *I* was the one she wanted out of her life, not her *Cheating. Best. Friend!*

"But not until she'd wrung the last drop of blood out of me. Not until she'd used me one more time. Not until after I slaved through her stupid dye crawl for her. Being charming to the simpering women who wanted a piece of her. Cleaning up after them when they spilled their filthy messes over the dye studio. *That's* when she was going to *get rid of me?*" She shouted.

She took a heaving, shuddering breath.

"That bitch thought she was going to get the best of me." A

manic grin split her lips. "Well, Special Agent Smith, I think not. Afterall, she's the one who's dead, and I'm—not. And you know what?" she asked leaning toward him.

"I'm not in the least bit sorry that I killed her." And throwing back her head, she laughed.

CHAPTER THIRTY

"Okay now that was *really* creepy, I didn't know about the tattoo," Janine said, when Wes finished recounting what had happened at the arrest site.

Grace's large orange cat purred loudly in her lap as she worked her fingers through its fur, a counterpoint to the quiet conversation going on around her.

Grace's parents had left Maisie there, and when Janine went back up to Meredith's, she would take the cat with her, like Grace had wanted.

They were sitting in Grace's pleasant, sunny kitchen—Wes and Harry, Janine and Dale Clay, and the sheriff with his bum leg propped up on the chair across from him, an ice pack balanced on his knee.

"Stood too long when Grace's folks were here," he said, wincing as he tried to get comfortable. "Poor people," he added. "They want to know what happened. And I wouldn't be averse to knowing all the details myself." He waved has hand before Wes could answer. "And yes, I know you're going to send me a written version in triplicate, no doubt, but why don't you give us the condensed version now."

That seemed fair enough, since as far as Wes was concerned, his part in the investigation was over. Weaver could take it from here.

A sentiment the man had echoed. He'd thanked Wes profusely for his help in bringing such a quick resolution to Grace Harper's murder, while telling him they'd give him a call if the case went before a jury and they needed his testimony.

Wes doubted that would happen.

He had a feeling the DA would offer a deal and that Ellen's lawyers would advise her to take it.

Leaning back in his chair, Wes looked around the table, and said, "So this is what I think happened.

"When Ellen left the barn this morning, she paused just outside the barn doors and heard Grace tell Meredith that she'd had enough of her. I think she was probably stunned and hurt and that she ran home, blinded by tears. Because in her mind they were partners. They'd had something precious together, and there was Grace just callously throwing it all away. Throwing *her* away.

"But I doubt the hurt lasted long. She probably didn't even make it across her kitchen before the rage set in. The kind of rage that makes you want to kill the person who just hurt you.

"Except, acting on that feeling, that's not something most of us would do. We'd just scream and yell and throw things. And be really hurt and angry. I think feeling betrayed would be in there somewhere, too.

"And that's what Ellen latched on to. That she'd been betrayed. That this glorious relationship she'd built up in her mind had just been—thrown away. And that seething anger? That wanting to kill the person who'd just hurt you? Became a real thing.

"I think if she'd still been near the barn, she would have stormed back in and attacked Grace right away. But she wasn't, she was at home, and the distance gave her time to think.

"More than likely, she was pacing around her living room, fuming, when she caught sight of that bag for Goodwill that had gotten left there. And I think, that without even thinking about it, she probably just picked it up and took it out to her front porch where she saw Dale Clay's car sitting in Grace's driveway."

"So she didn't really see it when she left the barn," Harry said nodding.

"No, I don't think so." Wes agreed. "I think she saw it right then, standing on her porch, and then Peter drove by, and she suddenly realized that she knew where Meredith was, too, and all the pieces of the puzzle just came together.

"She had the perfect alibi staring her in the face, if anyone thought to ask her."

"A crime of opportunity, through and through," Harry said, in disbelief. "Even down to the bloody shirt. All she had to do was reach into one of the bags at her feet and take out a shirt so she wouldn't get blood on the one she was wearing.

"Who would even think of doing that?" Janine asked.

"It could have been something as simple as she really liked the shirt she was wearing and didn't want to risk getting blood on it. Or she could have gotten the idea just because the bags of clothes were there, and she didn't care if she ruined one of them," Wes told her.

"Makes sense to me," the sheriff said nodding. "My wife keeps a couple of shirts to wear just for gardening, so she doesn't get any stains on her good ones."

Now that he'd mentioned it, Wes realized his mom did that too. Something to tuck away for future reference in case he and Harry ever got a place with a garden.

"So she, what, waited for Clay to leave before she killed Grace?" Janine asked.

"She didn't have to," the deputy said bitterly. "I pulled out right after that other Dodge Charger went by me."

"Huh. Funny she didn't mention seeing you too," the sheriff said, frowning.

"That's because I went the other way. I um, needed to get patrolling," he said, squirming slightly, avoiding the sheriff's eye by fiddling with his coffee cup.

Weaver blew out a breath but let it ride. And Wes had the feeling they'd already had that conversation and that the sheriff had ripped Clay a new one.

"Then she, what?" Janine asked. "Boldly walked back to the

barn, killed Grace, then went home, tossing the shirt in her burn bin on the way, and then went about her business like nothing had happened?"

"Pretty much," Wes told her. "Right after she took a trophy."

Which got both the sheriff's and deputy's attention.

"Yarn," Harry said, lip curling.

"Blood-splattered yarn, you'll find it in a yellow project bag, probably in her car," Wes told them.

"Okay, now that's just gone beyond horror movie scary," Janine said with a shiver. "But, wait. I thought you said whoever killed Grace splashed *dye* all over her yarn."

"They did. She did. I'm guessing grabbing up the dye and throwing it over the skeins was just the tail end of letting out her rage, but I bet there'll be splatters of blood on it too."

"From cast off," Weaver said nodding.

"Okay that's just—ew?" Janine said, squirming a little. "I can't even imagine wanting to touch yarn that had blood on it, let alone knit anything with it."

"Ellen said it was going to be a memorial to Grace."

"No. That's just wrong. So wrong," Janine muttered.

Wes wasn't going to argue about that.

"Then all she had to do was wait for the sirens," he finished.

"And once there was chaos in front of the barn, walk into the midst of it playing the part of Grace's good friend and neighbor. And everyone bought it," Harry added.

"Because what possible reason could Ellen Montrose have had to kill Grace?" Janine said with a snarl.

For a minute, it was quiet except for the cat's snorted breaths as she slept in Janine's lap.

"When did she set the shirt on fire?" the sheriff asked.

"It could have been anytime," Wes said, shrugging. "No one would have seen her. They were too fixated on the front of the barn. But it hadn't been burning long when we found it."

Then, with a huge sigh, Weaver said, "What a god damned shame. Grace Harper was a nice kid." He shook his head. "And I gotta admit, I liked Ellen Montrose too. She seemed like a real nice lady. Just goes to show you never know where crazy is hiding."

CHAPTER THIRTY-ONE

Speaking of crazy, that was the best word Wes could come up with when they got back to Daphne's.

Cars were jammed in every available space, packed door to door on the asphalt parking area. And Wes couldn't help feeling a little bit smug when he spied a spot no one had claimed yet, on the grass at the edge of the paved area, and wedged his SUV into it.

"Nice," Harry laughed, taking his hand as he helped her out.

"Not as nice as this," he told her, pulling her into his arms for a minute, hidden from view by the bulk of the vehicle itself and the hedge he'd parked next to.

"Hey, you," she said, kissing him on the chin.

"Hey," he answered, feeling better already, the tension of the day slipping away as he held her. Then sliding his lips across hers, he said, "I love you."

"That's good," she teased, eyes sparkling as she looked up at him, "because I love you too."

"Ready to go play with some yarn?" he asked her.

A smile lit up her face. "Can't wait."

"You know what, Red? Me neither."

"So, do you come bearing good news or bad news?" Daphne asked, coming up beside them as Harry held up two different skeins of worsted weight yarn for Wes's inspection.

They were standing against the far wall of Daphne's shop, under a sign that read "Worsted Weight. Good for sweaters, coats, jackets, slippers and blankets."

"Good," Harry told her. Then looking around to make sure no one could overhear her, she added quietly, "Wes caught the killer."

"Well, thank god for that. Was it—was it someone I might know?"

"Ellen Montrose," Wes told her.

Daphne shook her head. "No, that doesn't ring any bells."

"She was Grace's neighbor. She started out as a fan and ended up as a stalker."

"That's horrible! Poor girl," she added. "Honestly what is this world coming to when a yarn dyer has a stalker?"

Exactly! Wes thought, feeling a little more vindicated that he thought it had been weird, too.

"Well, congratulations on a job well and speedily done. And

if that yarn's for Wes, dear," she added to Harry, "then I'd go with the lighter gray color, or maybe this light steel blue? It picks up the color of his eyes so nicely." She handed Harry the yarn in question.

"It does!" Harry agreed, "How did I miss that one?"

"Easy enough to do with so many lovelies to choose from," Daphne said, smiling. "And now, after the events of the day, I imagine you're probably both ready to have a little fun."

Wes nodded. He was more than ready. "We're not too late, are we?" He glanced around at the almost empty shop around them.

"No not at all," she assured him. "As a matter of fact, we're waiting for one more couple to show up, so why don't you let Peter ring up your yarn sale, and then after, you can go on through into the dye studio where China will get you fitted out with smocks. And don't worry about your purchase, Harry, Peter will tuck it away behind the counter until you're ready to go home."

Then glancing out the window, she added, "Well, it looks like our stragglers are just pulling up, so if you'll excuse me while I go welcome them, I'll see you in the studio in just a few minutes.

"Oh, and Wes? Edgar can't wait to meet you during cocktail hour when we're done," she added.

"Someone's going to be going all fangirl," Harry singsonged.

"Will not," he told her. "All right, maybe just a little," he conceded when she raised an eyebrow at him.

Then, looking behind Wes, Harry gave a little giggle.

When Wes turned to see what was so funny, he couldn't help a laugh of his own.

"Did you know they were coming?" he asked, as his partner, Fountain Rhodes, and Fountain's girlfriend, Molly, stepped in through the doorway.

"Maybe?" Harry threw over her shoulder at him, grinning broadly, as she went to give Molly a hug.

Which meant, yes, Wes concluded with a little smile of his own, since the pair of them had become thick as thieves over the past year.

"Oh hi, guys!" Fountain said, with a little wave, not at all surprised to see them. "So, what have we missed so far?"

"A murdered dyer," Harry told him.

"And a deranged stalker," Wes added.

"So—nothing unusual for a fiber event?" Molly deadpanned, leaning in to give Wes kiss on the cheek.

"I can't tell if they're kidding or not," Fountain complained, head tipped to the side, as he studied them.

"Somehow, I doubt it," Molly told him, patting his hand. "And I, for one, am very glad we missed all the excitement."

"Well, I can see you're all old friends," Daphne said, smiling at the four of them, "and might I just say, a big welcome to Fountain and Molly. We're so glad you could come—and if you'll all follow me, now that everyone's here, we can get started."

"I'm really looking forward to this," Fountain whispered to Wes, as they donned their smocks and shoe covers.

A smile hovering on his lips, Wes told him, "Don't tell the girls, because I'll never live it down, but I am too."

"Was there really a dead dyer?" Fountain asked in a hushed voice, as they followed Harry and Molly over to where Daphne stood waiting to talk to everybody at once so the workshop could begin.

"Yeah, Grace Harper's neighbor stabbed her to death—I'll tell you about it later," he added, as Daphne began to tell them about all the various ways you could dye yarn and the ones they could choose to try in just a bit.

And as she spoke, Daphne's posh voice pulled Wes into a world where murder didn't happen, and he could make magic with only a small amount of skill of his own.

He made a different kind of magic with Harry much, much later.

But first they had cocktails with Daphne and her husband, Edgar, and then a lighthearted dinner with Fountain and Molly at a little Italian restaurant just down the street from their B & B.

Now, hours later, with a sleeping Harry in his arms, Wes lay watching the stars through the open curtains, thinking about the possibility of forever with her.

Snuggling Harry a little bit closer, he dropped a kiss on her cheek, and as he started to drift off to sleep, his last conscious thought was, but for now he was more than content to just enjoy being boyfriend and girlfriend, officially, for a while.

ACKNOWLEDGMENTS

I need to give a huge thank you to everyone who made this book possible.

To Barb Stone and Lisa Maltese for keeping my world running when I was down for the count – you guys are the absolute best.

To Natasha Laity Snyder of Unplanned Peacock who answered all my questions about dying yarn and dye studios, then sent me photographs of her own studio when I couldn't get there to see it in person – a million thank yous! And a million apologies for throwing it all out the window when it came time to write about it....

To my writing buddies – Babs and W. M.

And to my knitting buddies – Joy, Tracy, Beth, Stacy, Nicole, Linda and Cindy for putting up with me – again!

Special thanks to Madeline Farlow at Clause & Effect – for

everything! You make this whole adventure so much easier. I could not do it without you.

And, as always, to my guys – love you so much.

ABOUT THE AUTHOR

Hilary lives in North Carolina with her husband, who, sadly, does not want to talk about interesting ways to murder anyone. Her two grown sons, however, don't mind indulging their mom. A well-known knitting designer, best known for her enormous 'house cozy' shawls and hilarious MKALs (which you can find on her Ravelry knitting group Criminal Knits), she got into writing knitting mysteries because she felt the genre needed a little spicing up with some really hot guys, their zany girlfriends and a good dose of all knitterly things from an insiders perspective.

To Contact Hilary:
Criminalknits@gmail.com

CRIMINAL KNITS
for the serial knitter in all of us

THE KNITTING GAME

The Knitting Game is an online MKAL hosted by the author every few years on her Ravelry Group, Criminal Knits. The Traveling Scarf, featured in this book, was a previous Game that ran for 42 weeks . . . Yes, the author is insane.

Patterns connected to this book:

- The Dyeds of March

Patterns are available in my Hilary Latimer shop on Ravelry.

CRIMINAL KNITS

for the serial knitter in all of us